TEMPEST OCEAN

WN
NDS

DESERT

ODUSP
O
U
NIA
I
A

ange

OR

TEMPEST

OCEAN

MESMERIA
BRIGHTLAND

The Wand

Books by Allan W. Eckert

The Winning of America Series
The Frontiersmen
Wilderness Empire
The Conquerors
The Wilderness War
Gateway to Empire

Other Books
The Greak Auk
The Silent Sky
A Time of Terror
Wild Season
The Dreaming Tree
The King Snake
The Crossbreed
Bayou Backwaters
The Court-Martial of Daniel Boone
Blue Jacket
In Search of a Whale
The Owls of North America
Tecumseh! (Drama)
The Hab Theory
The Wading Birds of North America
Incident at Hawk's Hill
Savage Journey
Song of the Wild
Whattizzit?
Johnny Logan
The Dark Green Tunnel
The Wand
The Scarlet Mansion

The Wand

The Return to Mesmeria

by Allan W. Eckert

Illustrated by David Wiesner

Little, Brown and Company

BOSTON   TORONTO

First Edition

Library of Congress Cataloging in Publication Data

Eckert, Allan W.
    The wand.

    Summary: Back in the land of Mesmeria now under the rule of the evil King Krumpp, Lara and Barnaby discover all their friends imprisoned and the only way that they can rescue them is to find and learn how to use the secret volumes of the Warp and the Wand. Sequel to "The Dark Green Tunnel."
    [1. Fantasy] I. Wiesner, David, ill. II. Title.
PZ7.E1978Wan 1985   [Fic]   85-162
ISBN 0-316-20882-5

Published simultaneously in Canada by Little, Brown & Company (Canada) Limited

Printed in the United States of America

To the twins
who have gone through
The Dark Green Tunnel,
KRISTA AND SEAN VARIAN
. . . of Bellefontaine, Ohio.

Contents

The Wand

Prologue

Well, there *you are!*

Do you remember the twins, Lara and Barnaby?

What do you mean, no? Weren't you there when the story of their amazing exploits took place after they entered the Dark Green Tunnel?

You weren't? That's odd. I was sure I recognized you. Oh, I get it — you're just trying to fool me, aren't you?

Well . . . all right, all right! Just in case you weren't there for that exciting adventure, let me tell you just a little bit about it. You see, they had gone on vacation to Florida and went out into the Everglades in a boat with their cousin William. By a strange occurrence, they found a place where they were able to enter a remarkable world called Mesmeria. It was a place of remarkable beings, too — Fairies and Dwarves,

Elves and Centaurs, Tworps and Dwirgs and Gnomes . . . and even weirder and more dangerous creatures, such as crepuscular Krins and voracious Vulpines.

The twins and William got involved in some very serious trouble when, for reasons of his own, the reigning King wished to destroy them. And he very nearly did, too, but the twins and their cousin finally managed to get back to Florida. The problem then was that no one believed them and a storm had swept away the entry to Mesmeria. But the twins were sure their mother would believe them as soon as they told her on their arrival back in Chicago.

Now they are nearly there, but what happens turns out to be the most unexpected thing of all. . . .

A Most Unusual Rock

Lara and Barnaby were nearly home again.

The twins were about to discover, however, that being near was not the same as being home. Even though they were back at the same airport from which they had left for their vacation a month ago, something very unusual was about to happen that would delay their reunion with their family for a long time.

Perhaps forever.

In the big jet plane on the return trip from Florida to Chicago's O'Hare International Airport, the children had chattered at intervals about the astounding experiences they had undergone. "Do you remember . . . ?" one of them would begin, and off they would go on an excited discussion.

"Certainly I remember it!" Barnaby's answer was a bit short.

There was one question, however, that the twins kept coming back to that neither of them could answer: Would they ever be able to get back to Mesmeria again?

"I want to say 'Sure we will,' " Barnaby said, then added doubtfully, "but I just don't know."

"Well, I think we will," Lara said, but then she became unsure, too, and added, "Maybe. Some day . . . but I don't see how."

Naturally, once their plane landed and the children entered the huge airport terminal building, they were very excited at the thought of seeing their mother and stepfather again. They hurried along the crowded concourse toward the main building, where they were to meet them at the baggage claim area. There was a lot of noise and commotion: Announcements were coming over the loudspeakers and people were greeting each other, talking and laughing loudly. Others were rushing to get home or to catch their flights, and their feet clattered loudly on the tile floors.

It was no doubt because of all this confusion that the twins turned down the wrong corridor. Not until they had followed it around several corners did they realize that it was no longer crowded or noisy. They were all alone.

"Oh-oh," Barnaby said. "I think we've gone the wrong way."

The pair stopped and looked around and then at each other. Lara nodded. "I think you're right, Barnaby. Maybe we ought to turn around and go back."

Her brother shook his head. "I'm not so sure. What do you say we go on a little farther? Maybe if we turn down some more corridors we'll find the baggage claim."

"Okay."

They moved on, hand in hand, turning here and there as the corridor branched, becoming increasingly nervous. The light seemed to be getting dimmer and there was a growing dankness in the air. Their footsteps echoed hollowly and, almost unconsciously, they began to tiptoe. Barnaby was on the point of stopping and turning back, when there was a little exclamation from Lara.

"Look!"

Barnaby looked where she was pointing, first at the floor and then at the walls. No longer were they covered with gleaming, neatly laid tiles. Instead, the floor was of relatively smooth rock angling slightly downward and the walls had become gray and bumpy, even jagged in places. The lighting was very soft and came from luminescent clusters of lichens growing on the damp walls rather than from fluorescent tubes set in the ceiling, as before.

The twins turned around and gasped as they saw the familiar corridor was gone and they were now in a cave gradually disappearing in darkness ahead. There was also the hollow sound of dripping water. Barnaby began to tremble.

"I don't know what't going on, Lara," he whispered, "but I don't like it one bit. Mother and Father are going to be awfully worried if we don't show up soon at the baggage claim area."

Lara's eyes had become wide and round and she was gripping her brother's hand tightly, but she wasn't trembling. Not that she was braver, but because there was, for her, a certain familiarity about their new surroundings. Then the same feeling touched Barnaby.

"Do you suppose," he went on, "that somehow we've walked right back into Mesmeria without even knowing it?"

Lara considered this. "Well . . . I don't know. . . ." Her pulse quickened and she nodded. "I think you may be right! This is the same sort of tunnel I was in when I escaped from the Centaurs and first approached Twilandia. It's not *exactly* the same, but it's very much like it."

"You mean the tunnel you entered in the giant tree?" asked Barnaby. He was remembering what she had told him of her experiences after escaping from the cart in which they were being carried captive toward Castle Thorkin.

"Yes!" replied Lara, her excitement growing. "And if that's the case, then this is probably one of the five known tunnels that lead down to the cliff openings above

Twilandia. It's very much like the one where I met Krooom for the first time."

Barnaby's shivering subsided as he recalled Krooom, the giant diamond-patterned red-and-white snake Lara had met; the one on whose head she had ridden as the great serpent had flattened himself into a ribbon shape and flown down to the Mesmerian Underland called Twilandia.

"Do you really think so?" he said, smiling faintly. His earlier fear had faded and he, too, was growing excited. "If that's the case, then we probably don't have to be concerned about Mother and Father being worried."

Lara agreed, knowing Barnaby was referring to the fact that last time, though they had spent years and years in Mesmeria, they had discovered upon returning to Florida that hardly any time at all had passed while they were gone. "Sure," she said, "let's go on."

Now that they thought they knew where they were and where the tunnel led, their spirits had lightened considerably. There had been a lot of frightening occurrences when they went to Mesmeria last time, but the nice things far outweighed the bad. So now, still holding hands, they set off downslope, no longer afraid. Barnaby even began whistling a cheery tune as they walked, the sound echoing with happy hollowness in the chamber. Before long the tunnel turned downward at a steeper angle and the floor became even more damp and slick due to water dripping from the ceiling. Walking became difficult, and several times one or the other of the twins might have slipped and fallen, had not they been holding on to each other. Fortunately, just when it was becoming too treacherous a slope to follow safely, the floor changed to a broad flight of steps carved from the rock.

The steps, too, were damp and slick, but at least each step was level and it was easier to maintain balance. The tunnel curved and they continued downward for a hundred or more steps until there was an even sharper bend, and there the stairway ended. The twins sucked in their breath in wonderment at what was before them.

"Ohhhh!" breathed Lara, her eyes sparkling.

"Oh, *wow!*" gasped Barnaby.

The stairs had ended in a large chamber, at the other side of which was an arched passageway leading through solid rock, but that was not what had caused their re-action. From the ceiling of the chamber hung scores of pastel-colored stalactites — red, fuchsia, yellow, laven-der, beige, blue, mauve, green, orange, chartreuse, gold, purple, tan, aqua, puce, silver — each glowing with its own light. Similar formations were along the walls, while here and there on the floor of the cavern were stalag-mites in strange shapes and colors, also glowing. These stalagmites resembled thrones and robed figures, tables and weird animal forms. Wonderingly, looking this way and that, the children moved into the center of the room.

"It's . . . it's just *gorgeous!*" exclaimed Lara.

"It's . . . it's like standing in the middle of a Christmas tree," said Barnaby, turning around slowly to take it all in.

"Thank you," said a deep voice.

Lara looked at her brother. "Why did you say 'thank you'?"

"I didn't," Barnaby responded. "Didn't you?"

"Of course not. My voice isn't that deep."

"Well, then, if I didn't and you didn't, who did?"

"I did," said the same deep voice, causing the twins to spin around and stare at the source. The words had come from a rose-colored stalagmite — one of those that looked like a robed figure.

"A talking rock?" Barnaby said unbelievingly. "Stones can't talk."

"And why not?" retorted the stalagmite, sounding a bit hurt. "We have our rights, too, you know. I was merely being appreciative of the compliment. After all, we do have feelings. We change. We grow — slowly, to be sure, but we do grow. I hardly think our being able to speak justifies your rudeness and skepticism."

"Excuse us, please," said Lara hastily. "We meant no offense. We were just surprised. And we really are sincere in our admiration. You and your . . . your . . . friends are just beautiful. And I am forgetting my manners. Crobbity, Mr. —" She paused briefly, then added, "— I'm afraid I don't know your name."

"Crobbity to you," said the stalagmite, his voice becoming friendlier as he returned the traditional Mesmerian greeting. "I am — as are these others like me here — of the race known as Spelunkens."

"Actually," Lara said quickly, "I didn't mean what you and your people are called generally. I meant your own personal name."

"My, my, I don't ever recall being asked my *own* name before. Quite frankly, I don't even know for sure if I have one."

"Everybody has a name," Barnaby interjected.

"Well, obviously I'm *somebody,* since I'm standing here talking to you," replied the stalagmite. "Tell you what — why don't you just call me Rock?"

"Crobbity, Mr. Rock," Lara spoke up again. "We're pleased to meet you."

"Just plain Rock will do nicely, thank you. You are most kind. It is gratifying that you find us attractive. May I ask who you are?"

"My name is Lara, Rock, and this is my twin brother, Barnaby."

"I do not recollect hearing those names before."

"Perhaps," put in Barnaby, a trifle stiffly, "you heard of us by our proper titles, when we were here before, only a month ago — Queen Lara and King Barnaby."

The stalagmite was quiet for a moment, as if thinking. "No," he said at last, "I'm sorry to say it, but those names are unfamiliar to me. You must be mistaken about when you were last here. I've been standing here for

hundreds and hundreds of years and I've seen a lot of people come and go, but I've never heard of you."

"I don't understand, Rock," said Lara, her brow wrinkling. "Barnaby and I ruled Mesmeria for a great many years. We were part of a triumverate. Our cousin, King Daw, was the third."

"Ah!" said the stalagmite. "*Him* I've heard of, though not recently. I believe his reign ended somewhat over seven hundred years ago. Nothing but chaos since then."

"But how can that be?" Lara said, still frowning. "Something's very peculiar here."

"Not to me," Rock said in a bored manner.

"But it is!" Lara insisted. "Only a month ago we went from Chicago to the Everglades in Florida to visit our cousin and our aunt and uncle."

"Right," confirmed Barnaby. "Uncle Danny and Auntie Alice and our cousin, William."

Because Rock was acting so bored with all of this, he did not go on to explain that Uncle Danny was their *step*father's brother, so they weren't really related by blood to any of them. It just seemed as if they were. Besides, Lara was already talking again.

"And William took us out in his motorboat and we went into a sort of dark green tunnel in the mangrove trees and way out in the middle of nowhere we found a little beach with green sand."

"There was a turnstile on the beach," Barnaby interjected, "and so we went through it and we wound up in Mesmeria."

Lara confirmed this with a nod and added, "We found ourselves in the country of Verdancia. Do you know where that is?"

"I may not be swift, young lady," said Rock with a little edge to his voice, "but I'm not stupid. Naturally I know where Verdancia is, as well as the other countries of Mesmeria — Rubiglen, Selerdor and Mellafar. And, of course, the Underland country — Twilandia. I have to admit I've never *been* to any of them, but I certainly know where they are."

"Well it was in Twilandia that we fought King Thorkin and Warp, the Sorcerer," Barnaby explained, "and beat them."

"We —" Lara said patiently, "— the three of us — Barnaby and Daw and I — reigned in Mesmeria for many years. But when we went back through the Verdancia turnstile to visit with our families, we found we were children again and hardly any time at all had passed during our absence. We discovered that Auntie Alice and Uncle Danny didn't believe us. Before we could take them into the dark green tunnel to see for themselves, we had a big storm and the turnstile was lost, so we couldn't go back. We were going to tell our mother all about it when we got home, but we never *got* there because we walked down the wrong corridor in the airport."

Lara suddenly experienced a twinge of remorse at not feeling more concerned that her parents would be worried. She hoped they were right about time at home not passing at all while they were here, because this had all the signs of becoming another wonderful adventure.

Rock looked very uninterested at the explanation. He yawned widely and then said, "Well, thank you for stopping by. All this talking has made me very weary. I do believe I'll take a nap. Good-bye."

He became silent then, and though they tried to converse with him further, especially about his odd statement that King Daw's reign had ended over seven hundred years ago, there was no response. Finally, Barnaby became exasperated and turned away.

"It's like trying to talk to a rock," he grumbled. Lara laughed aloud at the inadvertent joke and, after a moment, he grinned. "Well, what now?" he asked.

"We head through that passage," Lara pointed at the arched opening, "and hope we find Twilandia on the other side."

Into Twilandia

LARA AND BARNABY walked boldly to the arched entryway of the passage through solid rock and stepped with equal boldness into that darkness. Within three steps, however, their boldness evaporated as the darkness closed over them like a glove. Behind them, the mouth of the tunnel glowed faintly from the soft light in the Spelunken's chamber. An even dimmer glow was barely visible far ahead, from the opening of the other end of the tunnel. But where they were it was absolutely black and only through reaching out blindly did they manage to find each other and tightly grip hands again. They were no longer so self-assured, but they still didn't want to turn back. Nevertheless, it *was* scary.

"Don't let go, Barnaby," Lara whispered in a quaking voice.

"Don't worry, I won't." He tried to sound brave but failed.

At every tiptoed step they expected something unseen to lunge at them. Their hearts beat very fast and so loudly that their imaginations made the whole tunnel throb with the sound. It took quite a time to walk that long dark way to where the tunnel finally opened out onto a broad ledge near the top of a terrifyingly high cliff. They walked to the edge and looked down. As they expected, far, far below — a mile or more beneath them — lay Twilandia, the Underland of Mesmeria.

The twins had been hoping this would be one of those ledges that had a narrow precipice trail angling down to the base, but it was not. This was the type of ledge from which, so far as they could see, only flying creatures could descend. The fact of there being no trail down was bad enough, but what made it much worse was the awful change in the land since last they saw it. The disappointment was so great that tears spilled from Lara's eyes and down her cheeks.

Twilandia had been a beautiful country of neat fields and shimmering blue lakes. Its capital city, Fir Tree, had been a thriving metropolis with alabaster-white buildings and brilliant green roofs, dominated by the awe-inspiring palace of Mag Namodder, she who was known as the Underland Witch and a very good witch she was.

And the whole of the land had been brightly lighted by the uniformly luminous clouds that lined the entire ceiling of the immense cavern.

Now those clouds were leaden, shedding only a gloomy light at best, like the threatening gray just before a heavy thunderstorm. What were previously neat and very pretty cultivated fields and orchards had been transformed into tangled, ugly overgrowth. As nearly as the children could judge from this height, the pretty white picket fences were gone and the low walls of green stone had been knocked over. Worst of all, the city of Fir Tree was largely destroyed. Here and there a few buildings remained with only minor damages, but the rest, including most of Mag Namodder's palace, were scarcely more than rubble overgrown with weeds.

Lara slumped to the ledge and lay there, shoulders heaving with her sobs. They had loved Twilandia and its people so much! Barnaby was no less affected, but he showed it in a different way — by becoming angry.

"We're going to find out who did this terrible thing, Lara," he said harshly. "We're going to find out what happened and where Mag Namodder is and where Daw is and what we can do to help them."

"How can *we* do anything?" Lara said, sitting up and wiping her eyes with the hem of her dress. "We can't get down there and we don't even know whether Mag Namodder and Daw are still alive."

"We *will* get down there!" Barnaby's flat statement

brooked no contradiction. "There's got to be a way and we're going to find it! C'mon," he held out his hand to her, "let's go back to the chamber and see if we can wake Rock. Maybe he can suggest something."

Lara nodded and took his hand and he pulled her to her feet. They turned back toward the tunnel entry and had no more than begun walking when they jolted to a stop. There, in the cliff face a dozen feet away from the tunnel, was a heavy wooden door reinforced with a latticework of iron bands. They ran to it and Barnaby tripped the heavy latch over the large keyhole, but the door refused to open. The boy pushed and shoved, grunting a great deal with his efforts, but it wouldn't budge. Lara added her strength to his, but to no avail. The door was securely locked and the twins finally gave up, gasping.

"Wait a minute," said Lara, stepping back. "We're forgetting that I attended the Magic One and Magic Two courses."

Barnaby nodded, remembering the time when Lara attended MSATM — the Mesmerian School of Applied and Theoretical Magic.

Lara continued without pause. "They were just basic and intermediate courses in spell-casting and I was a long way from qualifying for the Advanced Sorcery class, but I still remember a lot of it."

"The point is," Barnaby pressed her, "did you learn anything that could help us *here?*"

She thought about that and then smiled. "One of the intermediate spells I learned was —"

"The door-opening spell!" Barnaby interrupted. "But did you ever really cast it successfully?"

"Well," she was suddenly less sure of herself, "I passed the test okay, but all we had to open was a little cottage door. It was latched but not locked. It was a pretty flimsy door, too. Nothing like this one."

"Try it anyway," her twin urged. "You can do it, Lara. You can! At least you've got to *try!*"

She nodded and stood back about a dozen feet from the door, feet spread apart. For a long moment she stared at the door, her brow furrowed with concentration. Abruptly she screwed up her face until her eyes were so tightly squinched she could barely see, stretched her arm straight out and pointed her index finger at the door. In as stern a voice as she could muster, she invoked the spell.

"*Dehisce!*"

The faintest shimmering of the air by the door occurred, and then there was the groan of a heavy bar sliding and the clack of a lock tumbler moving and the click of the latch opening.

Smoothly and noiselessly, the heavy door swung inward.

Barnaby grinned, obviously impressed. Lara laughed aloud and clapped her hands together, pleased with herself. Together they ran to the door and looked inside.

It was a small square room, bare of furnishings. At the base of the far wall were four circular openings, each large enough for a person to enter. On the wall above the pair of openings on the left was a sign that said *RUBIGLEN* and another above the two on the right said *TWILANDIA*. Beneath these signs were two smaller signs, one above each of the openings, that read UP and DOWN. The two pairs of circular openings were separated by a pile of woven fiber mats above which was a smaller sign:

DIRECTIONS

1. Place mat in mouth of desired tube.
2. Sit down on mat. (Maximum: 2 people per mat)
3. Press START button.
4. Replace mat on pile at conclusion. (Warning: Do not stand while in motion. Keep hands and feet close to body.)

"Well, let's try it," Barnaby said. He took a mat from the pile and placed it neatly in the mouth of the Down-tube for Twilandia. At his direction, Lara sat on the mat with her legs outstretched before her. Barnaby sat directly behind her, a leg on each side and his arms about her. She leaned back against his chest.

"Ready, Lara?" Barnaby asked, a little thread of fear in his voice.

"Uh huh," Lara replied, not trusting herself to say more, since she was also very apprehensive.

On the side of the tube next to them was a little inset containing a red START button. Barnaby reached up and pressed it. Immediately there was a whirring sound and the floor of the tube began moving, carrying them forward. It would have been very dark in the tube except that at intervals of about every yard were three recessed green lights, one on the top and one on each side.

Suddenly the green lights before them angled downward very sharply. The whirring sound ended and they stopped on the brink. All was silence and then they slid into an almost sheer drop. Lara screamed as her stomach seemed to come up to her mouth, and Barnaby tightened his grip about her middle. Faster and faster they fell until the individual green lights appeared to become three solid green lines. The tube curved and banked and it was like being on a wild roller-coaster ride except that it was smoother and quieter and a whole lot faster.

Abruptly the tube leveled off and they could see the green lights stretching far in the distance ahead of them. The lights began angling gradually upward and their speed diminished. Far ahead there was pale yellowish light and they slid slower and slower as they approached it and finally came to a stop. The faint whirring sound came again and the floor of the tube moved, carrying them forward another twenty or thirty feet and gently depositing them in a room very similar to the one they had left.

"Wow!" Barnaby said. "What a ride!"

"I'll say," Lara agreed. "I wonder where we are now."

"We'll soon find out," her brother said, placing their mat on the pile nearby.

They looked at once for an exit and soon found it, but instead of being in the wall, the door was in the ceiling of the little room, reached by half a dozen stone steps. They climbed the steps, slid the heavy bar aside and pressed the latch, but the door remained locked. Once again Lara stepped back and invoked the Spell of *Dehisce*. There was a clacking sound as the lock tumblers moved inside the big keyhole and then the door swung open, inward and downward. They stared with surprise at the outer surface of the door, for it was coated with a thick layer of living grass. Cautiously they moved into the opening and stuck their heads outside.

They were at the top of a small grassy knoll easily half a mile from the cliff and not over a hundred yards from the ruins of Mag Namodder's palace. It looked to the twins as if they might be in what were once the beautiful gardens of that palace. A small square house halfway between them and the palace ruins was intact. Its walls were of stones fitted together with mortar, and there was a closed door and one window on the side facing them. The roof of the little house was coated with more living sod. Much closer to the children was a big smooth boulder jutting from the ground beside the doorway. It had a large symbol carved deeply into its surface — a circle with thin crossed lines through its middle and extending beyond the circle a little, like this:

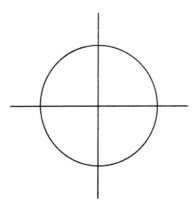

The twins stepped outside. Lara, still delighted with her magic abilities, turned and pointed at the rectangular hole in the ground from which they had emerged.

"*Occluda!*" she commanded.

The grass-coated door swung shut with a heavy thud and there was a click and a clack and a groan as it locked itself, becoming so perfectly camouflaged that had they not known the door was there, its presence would never have been suspected. It was evident that the symbol-marked boulder had been placed there to indicate the location of the hidden passage.

Before Lara and Barnaby had a chance to think about what they were going to do next, a heavy shadow flashed across them. There was a terrible shrieking cry, followed by a rush of wind that flattened the grasses around them and nearly bowled them over.

"Look out!" Lara shouted. "It's a Vulpine!"

And so it was — one of those huge, vicious, man-eating vulture-like creatures from the country of Dymzonia. He had whizzed by just over their heads on his great wings. These were extremely dangerous wings that had horny sawtoothed material lining the leading edges; wings that could easily cut a person in half. The Vulpine looked them over with expressionless amber eyes as he passed and then opened his huge, savagely-hooked beak and shrieked again. He banked sharply into a U-turn.

"He's coming back for us!" Barnaby yelled. "Run, Lara!"

Together they ran as fast as they could toward the little house, but they both knew they would never be able to reach it in time.

The Secret Volumes
of Warp

THE VULPINE WAS shrieking triumphantly as he closed the gap between himself and the twins. He was no more than five feet above the ground and only seconds remained before his cruel talons would grip them, when several things happened simultaneously:

As a voice from the little house shouted the word "*Impedo!*" there was a red flash at the window, a similar red flash at the Vulpine's head and a terrible crackling sound. Instantly the Vulpine fell, struck the ground and tumbled end-over-end. He came to a stop only a few feet from the children and lay there unmoving. Lara and Barnaby, who had been looking over their shoulders at the attacker as they ran, stopped and stared open-mouthed at the fallen enemy.

"Come inside! Quickly!"

The urgency of the voice caused the twins to spin around. An old wrinkled Dwarf with long white whiskers was standing in the now open doorway, beckoning. In his left hand was a crooked cane. They were so surprised they remained rooted in place.

"Hurry!" he said, his beard vibrating with his agitation. "Please! He'll awaken in just a few moments. You must get out of sight. Come inside!"

Barnaby grabbed Lara's hand and they ran toward the house. The Dwarf stood aside and the twins raced into the house together. Immediately he slammed the door and barred it. Then, leaning on his cane, he limped to the window. They joined him there, all sorts of questions bubbling up in their minds. Before they could say a word, however, he put a gnarled finger to his lips, silencing them.

"Say nothing!" he hissed. "The spell lasts less than a minute. If he doesn't hear you, he won't even remember why he's on the ground. Chances are he'll leave." They turned and looked outside from behind lacy curtains. Already the Vulpine was stirring and, as they watched, the predatory bird came woozily to his feet. He fluffed his greenish-black plumage and shook his head several times. Then he looked around curiously but paid no attention to the cottage. In a moment he turned, spread his great wings, took off with powerful wingbeats and rapidly disappeared from sight.

The old Dwarf released the breath he was holding. "He's gone. You had a very close call. Terrible birds. They're not at all bright, but they're deadly. We're safe from him for now." They saw now that in addition to the short cane of crooked wood in his left hand, he had a rather long, menacing-looking dagger in his waistband at his right side. He took off his floppy, cone-shaped red hat and grinned broadly at them, exposing small and very even white teeth. "Let me introduce myself. I am Quill. Now, tell me, who are you?"

"My name is Lara," said Lara.

"And I'm Barnaby," said Barnaby.

The Dwarf's bushy white eyebrows went up and his eyes widened. "Odd that you should have such names," he said.

"Why should that be odd?" Lara asked.

"Evidently your parents are students of history. Not many people these days even remember that once upon a time Mesmeria had two kings and a queen at the same time, all with equal power. One of the kings was named Barnaby and the queen was Lara."

"And the other king was Daw," piped up Barnaby.

"From Rubiglen," added Lara.

Quill nodded, smiling. "That's correct," he said, pleased and surprised that they knew. "I saw them once — all three of them together. I was in the crowd on hand the day that Queen Lara and King Barnaby passed through the Verdancia Turnstile and never came back."

"That was us!" Lara exclaimed. She was suddenly excited and, as many people do when they become excited, she began talking rapidly and her words ran together. "We meant to come back in just a few days," she went on, "but there was a storm and we couldn't find the turnstile anymore. We left Everglades and flew to Chicago and were going to ask our mother how to get back here, but we never did see her because while we were walking through O'Hare Airport, we were suddenly back in Mesmeria. But we were gone from Verdancia for only about a month."

Quill shook his head. "What you say confuses me. I know nothing about those strange places you've named, but I do know that King Barnaby and Queen Lara left

Mesmeria eight hundred and ninety-four years ago and they were, of course, adults then. You two are only children."

"You're right," Barnaby said, "it is confusing. Especially to us, because we definitely *are* the Lara and Barnaby who were Queen and King of Mesmeria."

"If that's true," Quill said slowly, by no means convinced, "then you could answer a few simple questions." He looked at them intently. His right hand moved toward the dagger in his waistband and there was an edge to his voice as he continued speaking. "Who was the leader here in Twilandia then?"

"Do you mean Mag Namodder?" Lara asked. "Her palace was right over there," she pointed in the direction where the palace ruins lay, "and I think this cottage we're in is where the palace gardens used to be. Or," she continued, reconsidering his question, "do you perhaps mean Menta, who was the leader of the Firtreans and head of the Superior Council and Mag Namodder's chief adviser?"

Quill nodded, but waved her question aside. "Who was general of the Twilandia Militia?"

"Rana Pipian," Barnaby interjected. "The warrior frog."

He nodded again. "And what was the name of the yellow bird who helped Lara and Barnaby?"

"Boggle!" the children said in unison.

"And how did Lara destroy King Thorkin?"

"I didn't destroy him," Lara protested. "He took my compact from me and looked inside and saw his own reflection in the mirror and that's what did it. I still have it, in fact. Look." She dug into the small pocket of her dress and extracted the little gold-colored plastic compact. "See," she said, snapping it open, "here's the mirror in this compartment, and here's the picture of my mother, Queen Enna, in the other."

Quill inspected it closely and handed it back to her, obviously impressed.

"It's extraordinary!" he said. "I do believe you *are* who you say you are. Welcome home, King Barnaby and Queen Lara. What an odd and remarkable circumstance that you should have returned as children."

"Yes, it is," Barnaby said, "and what bothers us most of all is what has happened here since we left. Twilandia was such a beautiful place. Why is everything ruined? Where is Mag Namodder? Where is King Daw? Where is —?"

Quill cut off Barnaby's rush of questions with an upraised hand. "Wait," he said. "There is so much we have to discuss. Let me get the cookies and pour us some hot tea and we can talk it all over."

That's exactly what they did. They sat at the little table and the twins drank butterscotch tea and munched crunchy cookies while the Dwarf spoke. Occasionally he stopped long enough to slurp his tea noisily, which Lara thought was not at all polite, but she politely overlooked it. The longer Quill spoke, the more upset and discouraged she and Barnaby became. Even though he was very concise in his narration, it took a long time to go over it all. This is what it amounted to in the end:

For many years King Daw had ruled wisely and well and his subjects were happy and prosperous. Eventually he married Roo-Too, who was one of the slender, red-haired, blue-skinned people called Tworps, from the Tworpestia District of Rubiglen. (Barnaby's eyes had lighted up at that because he had met Roo-Too.) Then — and Quill became very glum when he got to this part of his story — almost overnight, everything had changed. A powerful sorcerer named Krumpp invaded Mesmeria. He was from Bluggia, which was in the area of the world that was perpetually dark, just north of Dymzonia. Although that dark area was often called Darkland (just as Mesmeria was called Brightland because it was in perpetual daylight), its real name was Melanistica. It was made up of three provinces — Bluggia, Odusp and a large region called the Great Unknown Lands. Krumpp had planned his surprise attack well and, while his forces were sweeping across Mesmeria, he cast a spell on Mag Namodder that stripped her of her powers. Putting her in chains, he threw her into a dungeon presumed to be located on an island somewhere in Bluggia. King Daw, who had certain magical powers, was also made helpless, and he and Roo-Too were similarly imprisoned, presumably in the same place as Mag Namodder. The Darkland forces had by then swept all across the land, devastating not only Twilandia but also the four surface countries of Mesmeria — Rubiglen, Verdancia, Selerdor and Mellafar. What the twins had seen here in Twilandia was only a sampling of similar devastation elsewhere.

Tears were running down Lara's cheeks when Quill finished, and Barnaby was sniffling a little.

"Well, are Mag Namodder and King Daw and Roo-Too still alive?" Lara asked, hiccuping. (She very often got hiccups when she cried.)

"Assuming they haven't been killed, there's no reason why they shouldn't be," Quill replied seriously. "After all, it was only about seven hundred and fifty years ago and their life span, barring misfortune, should be two or three times that."

"Then there must be *something* we can do to help them," Lara said. "Can't we try to rescue them?"

"Many have tried, Your Majesty," said Quill, rubbing a hand across his bald head. "None have succeeded and most have never returned."

"Please," Lara said quickly, "just call us Lara and Barnaby. It's obvious we're not a king and queen anymore and just our names will do very well."

"Thank you, Your Maj——" he caught himself and amended, "— Lara. To go on, there are terrible dangers that we know of and probably many others, perhaps worse, that we don't even suspect. Rana Pipian led one of the first rescue parties, comprised of thirty of our strongest and best. Only one returned — a Centaur named Cupper. He was badly hurt and died soon after, but he lived long enough to tell us that the party had successfully passed through Dymzonia and into southern Bluggia. Then they were attacked and Rana Pipian was captured. Whether or not he was executed after that, Cupper didn't know. Except for Cupper — and perhaps Rana Pipian — all the others in the party had definitely been killed during the retreat, not only by unspeakable monsters in Darkland, but by the voracious Vulpines and crepuscular Krins in Dymzonia."

"We have to do *something*," Lara persisted.

The Dwarf put down his teacup and stroked his whiskers for a long moment, his brow wrinkled with concentration. Then the wrinkles faded away and he looked closely at them.

"There may be one slim hope. You wouldn't happen to know where the *Secret Volumes of Warp* are hidden, would you?"

Lara shook her head, but Barnaby leaped to his feet, bumping the table and nearly upsetting the teapot and cups.

"I know!" he cried. "Daw told me about them. When he and I were put under the Spell of *Ossyfia* and paralyzed from the neck down, Daw managed to partly lift the spell off himself. He was able to do that because he told me he had read a little on it in what he called the

33

Spell Books belonging to Warp. He found them in a
hidden room in the castle. You know where Castle
Thorkin is, don't you?"

"Yes," Quill, replied, "I do, though I've never been
inside. Please go on."

Barnaby cleared his throat and continued. "As I said,
the books belonged to Warp, King Thorkin's sorcerer.
Warp kept them in a secret chamber in one of the towers, along with a strange-looking magic wand. One day
Daw followed him and learned how to get inside. He
said he went into the room by himself only once and
started paging through the *Secret Volumes* — there were
three of them — but he was nearly caught by Warp and
wasn't able to finish. He did tell me where the hidden
room was, though, and how to get in. I always meant
to go there and browse through the books, but somehow
never really had the time."

"Barnaby!" It was Lara, looking a little miffed. "You
never told me about that."

He shrugged and looked chagrined. "I meant to," he
said. "I guess I forgot."

Quill was staring at Barnaby. "You really *do* know
where the *Secret Volumes of Warp* are hidden? Then that's
the only hope. Those books contain the knowledge of
some of the most powerful magic spells known. I know
nothing about the wand you mentioned, but if Warp hid
it there, it must have great powers of some sort." He
shook his head and one of his shaggy brows lifted. "Cas-

tle Thorkin is controlled by King Krumpp's forces now, but we must get past them somehow and look at those books. I don't know a great deal of magic, but with what I do know, if there's a way to rescue Mag Namodder and the others, it will be written in them." His gaze took in the twins. "Are you both willing to try? It might be dangerous."

"Of course we will," Lara said instantly.

And with those words the matter was settled and the quest was begun.

4

The Quest Begins

QUILL, HELPED BY Lara and Barnaby, quickly tidied up. As soon as the cups and saucers were washed, things put away and the cookies placed in a little pouch which the Dwarf slung over his shoulder, they left the house and walked to the symbol-marked boulder by the hidden door. Quill, despite his limp — the result of an injury he had suffered from the whiplike tail of a Krin during Krumpp's takeover of Twilandia — moved along quite well. (The crepuscular Krins, as you may recall, are the large, ferocious lizard-like creatures from Dymzonia, with armored scales, huge teeth like an alligator's, and a dangerous tail like a bullwhip.) It was when they stopped near the boulder that Quill reached into a pocket of his vest and extracted a little wooden tube. It was a whistle with three finger holes.

"Once we get to Rubiglen," he said, "we're going to need some swift transportation and almost surely some help. I'll take care of that right now."

He put the whistle to his lips and his cheeks puffed out as he blew three shrill notes, each of a different tone. The sound echoed through the nearby hills and soon the Dwarf smiled and pointed.

"Ah," he said, "here they come."

The twins looked where he was pointing and saw three large birds heading toward them, low to the ground. For an instant they were afraid these were more of the voracious Vulpines, but then Lara let out a happy cry and clapped her hands together.

"They're Kewprums!" she said, remembering with fondness the beautiful hawk-people they had known here in Twilandia.

The three birds sailed in gracefully and alighted gently in the grass before them. Each was as large as a man, with plumage the color of brushed copper.

"You called?" said one, who was evidently the leader.

"Yes, Kite," said Quill. "Thank you for coming so quickly. These two," he dipped his head toward the twins, "despite the fact that they are children in form, are Queen Lara and King Barnaby, returned to us at last from Other World."

All three Kewprums were obviously overwhelmed at the news and they bowed low simultaneously.

"Your Majesties," said Kite as he straightened, "how good it is to have you back. I am, as Quill has said, Kite. My companions are my wife, Kestra, and our nephew, Phalco." The two, who had also straightened, bent their heads respectfully as they were introduced. Kite continued, "Does your return mean you intend to depose that rascal, Krumpp, and resume your rule again?"

"That is why I've summoned you," the white-bearded Dwarf interjected. "We hope that will eventually be the case. At the moment, we are about to set out on what will most likely be a perilous mission and I wish to know if you are free to help us."

"What is the nature of this mission, Quill?" asked Kestra, her voice clear and lovely.

"We will need transportation from the other end of the tubes," he indicated the hidden doorway with his thumb, "to Castle Thorkin in Verdancia. We may encounter enemies on the way and almost certainly when we get there. We intend to enter the castle — by stealth, if possible. That may not be possible at all. Thus, if we are discovered, there may be fighting. It could very well be fatal. In light of that, are you willing to help?"

"Without a doubt, if it is to aid Queen Lara and King Barnaby," said Phalco promptly. "They were friends of my great-grandfather, who once was a member of the

Superior Council. He was killed during the battle fought against Thorkin at the Twilandia Cliffs."

"Really?" said Lara, suddenly excited. "That must have been Kreee. He was such a wonderful person."

"Yes, he was, Your Highness," said Phalco. "Unfortunately, I did not get to know him as well as I would have liked. I was only one hundred and twelve years old when he was killed."

"One further question," Kite put in. "It has no bearing on whether or not we will go, since we certainly shall, but what is the purpose of your going right into the very jaws of the enemy, as it were, by attempting to enter Castle Thorkin unnoticed?"

"We hope," Quill said, "to find the *Secret Volumes of Warp*. And a wand that is supposed to be hidden with them. If we do, we will find what we need in those books."

"Which is?" prompted Kite.

"Information that may allow us to discover not only the whereabouts of Mag Namodder, but perhaps also the knowledge we need to set her free."

There was a stunned silence as the impact of Quill's words struck the three coppery birds. Then it was Kestra who spoke.

"Had there been any doubt in our minds before about accompanying you — which there wasn't — there would be none now. We are with you without reservation."

"To the death, if need be!" said Kite.

"Aye!" agreed Phalco.

With that, Quill pointed his crooked cane and invoked the Spell of *Dehisce*, opening the sod-covered door. All six filed down into the chamber. Although she didn't say so, Lara thought she was able to cast a much smoother *Dehisce* spell than Quill, without even having to use an implement to do so, and she couldn't help feeling a little smug.

With the door closed and locked behind them, they picked up three mats from the pile and entered the tube marked RUBIGLEN. Two-by-two on the mats — first Quill and Kite, then Lara and Barnaby, and finally Kestra and Phalco — they took their places. When they were settled and ready, Quill reached out and pressed the red START button. Immediately a deep roaring began, quickly growing in volume. There was suddenly a great wind, not from behind, pushing them, but from in front, pulling them with tremendous suction.

"It's like a giant vacuum cleaner, Lara," Barnaby yelled close to his sister's ear.

It was the last any of them said for a while, since the sound became much too loud to speak over. The mats began sliding forward, slowly at first but then with increasing speed. The spaced lights on the sides and roof of the tube were red. By the time the travelers began angling upward, their speed had increased so much that the lights had become three solid lines of red.

At the midway point they were gently deposited in the chamber where Lara and Barnaby had begun their slide down to Twilandia. Without delay they took their places in the other half of the RUBIGLEN tube and completed the journey without incident. For the twins, the ride up had been every bit as exhilarating as the ride down and they were giggly and their eyes dancing with excitement when they emerged from the hidden opening in Rubiglen. The sky was cloudless green, as they had known it would be, and the warm green sun was shining brightly.

The opening from which they had emerged was almost identical to the one in Twilandia, even to the boulder marked with the symbol $\oplus$. They found themselves atop a knoll covered with lilac-colored grass situated on a point of land stretching westward into a quite sizable body of water.

"That's Amethyst Lake," Quill told the twins. "You were probably here more than once during your reign."

Both Lara and Barnaby nodded, and Barnaby pointed to the other side of the lake, where a shoreline was just barely visible.

"Over there is where Daw City is located, right?" The Rubiglen capital city was named after their cousin, King Daw.

"Right," Quill said. "Now, I suggest we get about our business."

With the door shut and locked behind them, Quill

climbed on Kite's back, hooked his knees over the leading edge of the bird's wings where they joined the body, and took a good grip on the neck feathers. Lara followed his example on Kestra's back and Barnaby was soon in place on Phalco.

"Aren't we awfully heavy on you?" Lara asked the Kewprums generally. "I mean, for you to fly with us on your backs?"

All three of the birds laughed aloud, but it was Kestra who replied: "No, indeed, Your Majesty. Actually —"

"Please," Lara interjected, "we'd like it if all of you would just call us Barnaby and Lara."

Kestra bowed her head respectfully. "Thank you, . . . uh . . . Lara. You honor us. What I was saying was that, actually, we could carry three apiece, if necessary. However, with only one each, we'll still be able to maneuver and fight quite well if we should happen to be attacked by Vulpines."

Quill's eyebrows went up like fluffy little clouds on his brow, which Lara had discovered meant he was ready to say something, so she nodded at him.

"I suggest we come in low from behind the Gray Mountains, Kite," the old Dwarf said, "and land in the forest just out of sight of the castle. We can then slip up and study the situation at the castle from under cover."

"That," Kite said, "is a very good idea — a reconnaissance." Kestra and Phalco nodded in agreement.

Immediately the three birds took off, Kite in the lead,

with Phalco and Kestra a wing-length apart just behind
him. And while the ride through the tunnel had been
exhilarating for the twins, it could not compare with the
wonder and enjoyment of this ride.

They quickly climbed above the trees and then the
Kewprums used warm air currents — convection currents, Kite called them — to glide in circles to such a
height that soon they could see the whole form of Amethyst Lake stretched out below them. At a sharp command from Kite, they stopped gliding and flapped with
strong smooth strokes to the southeast. Before long they
were flying southward along the range of peaks called
the Ruby Mountains.

For over two hours they flew, and the beautiful coun-
tryside of lavender woodlands and rust-colored prairies
and green lakes and streams unrolled beneath them. The

beauty, however, was limited to the unpopulated areas. Whenever they neared cities or towns, there was nothing but ruins overgrown with briers.

"Where are all the people?" Lara asked. "The Fauns and Gnomes and Tworps and Dwirgs, along with the Dryads and Nyads and Centaurs and Dwarfs and all the others? Where is everyone? I haven't seen anyone at all."

"Underground, most of them, I suspect," Kestra replied. "That's where they moved to for safety when the cities were destroyed. If Krumpp knew where these hidden communities were located, he would destroy them. But that's not the only reason you're not seeing anyone. There are too often Vulpines flying about for anyone to be safe walking around in the open. Far more here, in fact, than in Twilandia. Sometimes the Mesmerians venture out, but only with great care. Everyone is very much afraid, as they have been ever since Krumpp conquered us. I'll be very frank with you — we can consider it fortunate that we *haven't* seen anyone, because anyone we might see moving about conspicuously would almost surely be one of Krumpp's occupation force."

After more than three hours of flying, the Gray Mountains of Verdancia appeared far ahead, jutting into the sky like fangs. The Kewprums swept lower then, angling westward to go around the mountains and approach them from the southwest. Within another quarter-hour they were skimming close to the trees in heavily forested passes of the mountains. As they crossed the highest ridge, they glimpsed, ahead and below, the sprawling inland sea known as Green Lake. And dead ahead, in that instant before they dipped into the trees on the downslope, they had an even briefer view of the tiny island close to shore, upon which stood Castle Thorkin.

Five minutes later they landed in a dense section of woodland on steeply sloped ground. Following Quill's example, Lara and Barnaby dismounted, marveling over the fact that the great birds were not in the least winded from their efforts.

"No more talking now," Quill warned, "and no noise. Watch out for dry branches that might snap underfoot. We mustn't give ourselves away."

Afoot and in single file, with Quill limping along in the lead, they moved downhill until only a final screen of brush separated them from a clear view of the castle. Carefully they spread the branches apart just enough to see. There, only a few hundred feet ahead, was the looming gray-rock bulk of Castle Thorkin, its multitude of towers and turrets rising high above them. On each turret flew a red flag with a wavy blue line running diagonally through it — the banner of King Krumpp.

A line of guards armed with spears and swords stood an arm's length apart, stretching outward from the castle across the drawbridge and a hundred yards beyond that on the narrow causeway leading to the mainland. Lara and Barnaby looked at one another and there was

no longer any sign of lightness or excitement or antici-
pation in their eyes. So far as they could see, there would
be no possibility of getting inside Castle Thorkin unseen. They looked at Quill, eager to hear his plan for
gaining entry, but his whisper made a sudden chill run
up their backs.

"Well," he murmured, taking off his cone-shaped
floppy red hat with one hand and scratching his shiny
bald pate with the other, "what do we do now?"

5

The Shrood

Q UILL, LEANING ON his cane, looked considerably embarrassed at having to admit that now they were here before Castle Thorkin, he really didn't know what to do. He simply hadn't thought that far ahead and, as many of us do, had impulsively set things in motion without any real plan. He was clearly stumped and that was what had prompted him to say, "Well, what do we do now?"

"We could fly in and land on the roof," whispered Phalco.

The other two Kewprums — Kestra and Kite — merely shook their heads and looked at Quill expectantly. They thought his question was merely rhetorical. *Surely* he had a plan. Why else would he have summoned them to serve in this dangerous mission?

"Maybe we could swim across to the back side of the island and find a secret entrance," said Lara in a hushed, hopeful voice.

Barnaby was much taken aback by Quill's unexpected remark. He frowned and changed position, moving closer to the wrinkled old Dwarf. More than just a little angry, he was about to whisper sharply at Quill that, having taken over leadership of the party, it was Quill's responsibility to come up with a workable plan of some kind. Before he could even open his mouth to speak, someone beat him to it.

"Hey! Watch where you're stepping, you big oaf!" The uncommonly deep voice came from somewhere near Barnaby's feet.

The boy looked down and the other members of the party followed his gaze. Very close to his right foot, reclining on his back on a little patch of soft, brilliant green moss, was an extremely small mouselike creature with eyes not much bigger than a typewritten period. He had fine, pale gray fur, a head that was greatly elongated and a small black button of a nose at the end of his sharp muzzle. His ears were hardly more than little holes to the rear of his eyes and he had a short, faintly fuzzy tail. His hind legs were comfortably crossed and his forelegs were bent back with the paws interlocked behind his head.

Obviously he had been resting, but now, just as obviously irked over being disturbed, he came to an upright position on his hind feet. He smoothed his garb — a sort of knee-length robe, similar to a Roman toga belted at the waist — and then placed his forepaws on his hips and glared at Barnaby.

"You are approximately four feet seven inches tall and of moderate physical stature, which suggests, through deductive logic, that your weight is in the vicinity of sixty-five pounds. All that weight is concentrated, as you step, on one foot, which means that enough pounds per square inch are generated to have caused a substantial compression on a body such as my own should placement of your foot have been only a little closer."

"Huh?" said Barnaby.

"In other words, another half an inch and you would have mashed me with those gigantic clodhoppers of yours," he said in his baritone voice, pointing at the boy's nearest foot. "Of course," he added, shrugging, "everyone's stepped on me all my life, so why shouldn't you?"

"I'm . . . I'm so sorry, sir," whispered Barnaby, stammering because he was still so surprised at discovering this minute creature whose voice was so deep. "I didn't see you there," the boy went on. "You . . . you're very tiny." Then he added hurriedly, "Meaning no offense, of course."

"Sure, sure," snapped the animal in the red toga, his eyes bright with anger. "Little guys always pay the price, don't they? No one ever means any offense until they offend and then they're soooooo sorry!" He spread out his forelegs in an exaggerated gesture.

"You look like a . . ." Barnaby paused and then began again. "Well, excuse me, but you look very much like a shrew." He was remembering the pictures he had seen, in nature books in the school library, of the smallest mammal in the world. "Is that what you are? A shrew?"

"Well, well," said the little creature, "there may be some hope for you yet. Most people who see me for the first time — and that doesn't happen very often, I assure you — think that I am a mouse." He stuck out a tiny pink tongue and made a "Blyckk!" sound, then added, "Imagine, mistaking *me* for one of those disgusting, stupid cheesebrains! The smallest mouse is three times bigger than I, and a thousand times more stupid." He paused and bowed slightly. "I, my dear sir, am a Shrood. We are not a numerous race and I am led to believe — however distasteful it may be to contemplate — that we evolved from the shrews. But Shroods are infinitely more intelligent. Indeed, yes."

"We regret having disturbed you, Mr. . . . ?" Quill put in softly.

"Ergot, is the name. E–R–G–O–T," he added, spelling it out, "but the *T* is silent, as in escargot. Just plain Ergot. And why should you regret having disturbed me? Everyone else disturbs me, so why —"

Quill interrupted. "Please excuse me again for interrupting you, Ergot, but we do not have time to stand here nattering. We are on serious business."

"Oh, just go ahead, interrupt me!" Ergot snapped. "You won't be the first, you know. Sooner or later everybody interrupts —" Abruptly he broke off and gave Quill a more penetrating look. "Serious business, you say? Whoops! See there, I told you so! Even *I* interrupt myself. It's always the way. All right . . . serious business? What's the nature of your serious business?"

"Well, now," Quill said, still speaking in a whisper. "I don't believe I can tell you that. After all, you are a perfect stranger to us."

"Thank you, sir, thank you. Yes, I am perfect in virtually every way. Even as a stranger, I am a *perfect* stranger." He frowned. "That doesn't make me a bad person."

"I did not say you were a bad person," Quill protested, his words barely audible. "Only that you are a stranger to us and that our business is private and does not concern you."

"Your business," Ergot mused in a soft voice. "Hmmm, your business . . ." His eyelids half closed for a moment as he considered this. Then they popped open and he stared at the Dwarf. He cleared his throat and spoke distinctly. "Why is it that you six, who are enemies of the powerful sorcerer Krumpp, have embarked so hurriedly on your terribly important quest and come all the way from Twilandia in an attempt to get inside Castle Thorkin?"

Lara was shocked. "How in the world," she blurted in a harsh whisper, "do you know we want to get inside Castle Thorkin?"

"And how do you know we are enemies of Krumpp?" muttered Barnaby.

"And how do you know we are from Twilandia?" Kestra put in softly.

"And how do you know," Phalco demanded, whispering as the others had, "that we left Twilandia in a hurry?"

"Yes," Kite said, just as quietly, "and, equally, how do you know we are on an important quest?"

Ergot sighed in an exasperated way. "I just can't understand why it is," he said, "that people are always asking me 'Why did you say *this*?' or 'How did you come to know *that*?' It's all so elementary!"

"Answer our questions," Quill hissed menacingly, touching the haft of the dagger at his waist, "or I'll slice you in half!"

"Tsk, tsk, tsk," clucked Ergot, shaking his head sadly. "Threatening me, are you? I guess you might as well. Everybody else threatens me, so why should you be any different?"

Quill's hand flashed out and snatched up the Shrood by the tail, gripping it between thumb and forefinger. His dagger had miraculously appeared in his other hand.

He dangled Ergot in front of his own face, and touched the sharp, narrow point of the weapon to the Shrood's stomach.

"I warned you!" he gritted. "How do you know we're afraid? Speak up and answer the questions — all of them! This is your last chance."

"All right, all right," Ergot said. "If you must have everything spelled out for you, it's simply a matter of fundamental logic. Since you are obviously not tired and your feet are not scuffed from contact with the rocky terrain and your clothing is not torn from the brambles you would have had to walk through to get here, the logical assumption must be that you did not come here on foot. And, since you have Kewprums with you," he dipped his head at Kite, Kestra and Phalco, "it is most likely that you flew here on their backs. Now — it's common knowledge that Krumpp has virtually wiped out the Kewprum population in all countries of Mesmeria except Twilandia, so these three must be Kewprums who still live in Twilandia, where Krumpp's control is not so strong. This being the case, it is evident that all of you came from Twilandia. Furthermore, you have almost no equipment or supplies with you, meaning that the reason you came here was so urgent that it left no time to bother with such things. That, of itself, bespeaks a most important and urgent quest."

Ergot paused, looking Quill full in the face, and then continued in a level tone. "You are fearful, otherwise you would not be whispering. If, therefore, you are fearful, it means you are afraid of *something*. Obviously, it is not of each other, nor of me, so let's analyze it: You are hiding behind bushes, so you are fearful of being seen. You do not wish to be seen by anything or anyone on the other side of those bushes. King Krumpp's guards are on the other side. Therefore, you fear being seen by those guards. If you fear being seen by the guards, you evidently fear that if they saw you, they would catch you. And if you fear being caught, it is most probably because you fear they would take you before Krumpp. Now then, if you were a friend of Krumpp's, you would not be afraid of being seen and caught and taken before him. Since you *are* afraid of being seen, it follows that you are *not* a friend of Krumpp's. Thus, it is Krumpp you fear; his guards are only extensions of that fear. And since you fear Krumpp and do not want to see him or have him see you, yet you are here at Castle Thorkin where he has his headquarters, it thereupon follows that Krumpp is your enemy and the object of your important quest is inside Castle Thorkin and that is where you wish to go. You see, it's all so elementary."

All six members of the party were speechless at Ergot's flawless logic.

The Shrood took advantage of the moment by swinging himself up onto Quill's thumb, carefully disengaged his tail and then perched there on the back of the Dwarf's hand. His long snout wrinkled as he licked his forepaws and cleaned his whiskers with them in a very self-satisfied way.

They watched him as if in a trance. When finished, he straightened and grinned, then addressed them again, quietly and calmly, in his strangely deep voice.

"I hasten to assure you," he said, "that Krumpp is very much my enemy, too. Not only for what he has done to Mesmeria and to Mag Namodder and our good leaders, but on a more personal level as well. Shortly after he came here, he was striding through these woods and almost stepped on my brother. When my brother yelled at him to watch where he was going, Krumpp deliberately turned around and stamped on him. And then, when my brother's wife screamed and ran to what was left of her husband, Krumpp laughed and crushed her in the same way. He is a very bad man. I have sworn vengeance against him, but he is large and powerful, while I am very small and weak. I cannot take my vengeance alone, but I will be satisfied if I can aid others in such a matter. And, mark what I say, I *can* be of considerable value."

Ergot bowed very deeply, then straightened. "I am," he concluded, "at your service."

It was Lara who responded first. She held her hand out beside Quill's and the Shrood leaped onto her palm and dipped his head toward her respectfully, then waited for her to speak.

Lara politely said, "Crobbity, sir," and introduced

herself and the other five. Then she added gently, "We appreciate your generous offer and we mean no disrespect, but we're not after revenge. We just want to rescue Mag Namodder and King Daw and Queen Roo-Too. And our friend, Rana Pipian, if he's still alive. And perhaps if we *can* rescue them, then they may be able to force Krumpp to return to where he came from and Mesmeria can once again become the beautiful place it used to be."

Ergot nodded and momentarily hung his head. "I am ashamed," he murmured. He looked up at her. "It was my anger speaking. You are, of course, correct. To seek vengeance is a very bad thing; in its own way, almost as bad as outright evil. As of this moment, your goal is mine — I will help you and your friends in any way I can."

"But what could a little . . ." Barnaby paused, trying to find the word he wanted. "What could a little individual like *you*," he continued, "possibly do to help *us*?"

Ergot proudly drew himself up to his full height of one-and-a-half inches and spoke grandly.

"I will get you into Castle Thorkin unseen by anyone."

6

Into Castle Thorkin

WITH ERGOT GIVING directions, Lara carried him the
twenty yards or so to the base of a large tree where there
was a tiny hole, which was where he lived. The others
followed closely and watched as Lara set him down.

"I have something inside my quarters that will enable
us to enter Castle Thorkin unseen," he told them. "Wait
here. I'll be back in a minute."

With a jaunty flick of his minuscule tail, he ducked
into the hole. When he said he would be back in a
minute, he was not generalizing. In precisely sixty seconds he reappeared, a pouch no larger than your
thumbnail slung over his shoulder.

"I told you earlier that people rarely see the Shroods,"
he said, his deep voice rumbling softly in the little hid-

den glen where they were gathered. "Part of the reason is because we are so small. But even more than that," he dug in his pouch and extracted a milk-white fungus not much larger than a grain of rice, "we eat these *topa* mushrooms."

He took a bite from the fungus and instantly his entire form, including the clothes he was wearing and the pouch he carried, became momentarily misty and then disappeared.

"He's gone!" exclaimed Barnaby unnecessarily.

"Not gone," came the deep voice of Ergot. "Just no longer visible. I'm still right where I was. Please don't move about or you might step on me."

"Oh, how wonderful to actually become invisible!"

Lara breathed, speaking to the empty place where the Shrood had been standing. "How long does it last, Ergot?"

Even as she spoke a second mistiness occurred and in another moment the Shrood reappeared, standing exactly where he had been before. "Not long, if you take only one bite, as I did," he explained. "But one whole *topa* will keep me invisible for about half an hour."

"That's wonderful!" Quill said. "Now all we need is a large enough supply of them to last us until we can get into the castle, find what we want and get out again. Where do we get more of these *topa* mushrooms, Ergot?"

The Shrood shifted uneasily. "Well, we have a little problem there," he admitted. "The *topa* grow underground and they're very hard to find. I have four sacks like this," he patted his shoulder pouch, "filled with them."

They then discussed how long the invisibility would last on a larger person and quickly tested it. Since Barnaby was the only one who knew where the *Secret Volumes of Warp* were hidden, it was obvious that he would have to be one of those who would enter the castle. He popped one of the little mushrooms into his mouth, chewed it up and swallowed. Almost immediately he vanished, but the results were disappointing. He reappeared less than five minutes later. Barnaby estimated that it would take a minimum of an hour to accomplish their mission if they weren't detected, and so they did some rapid calculations and were distinctly disappointed with their conclusion: Ergot's entire stock of *topa* was only enough to permit two of them to remain invisible for somewhat less than an hour. It was hardly sufficient time to get in, locate the hidden volumes and get out with them, but there was no alternative.

"Now," Quill said, "we have to decide who's to go with Barnaby."

"I think it should be one of us," said Kite, speaking for the Kewprums. "We're expert fighters, if it comes to that, and he may need protection. I volunteer to go with him."

"So do I," said Kestra.

"Me, too," added Phalco, eagerly.

"Well," Quill said, shaking his head, "it seems to me that I should go with him, since not only could I help protect him," he patted the dagger in his waistband, "but I know a little magic already and would be able to decide which of the spells in the *Secret Volumes of Warp* could be of greatest value to us."

"No," said Lara firmly, shaking her head. "if Barnaby goes, I go too. I may not know as much magic as you," she told the Dwarf, "but I do know *some*. Besides, we may need you and the Kewprums outside to help rescue us if we run into trouble."

"But you're just a girl!" Quill objected.

Lara stamped her foot angrily. It was a silly argument

that she had heard too many times already. "Chauvinist!" she flared, not caring that Quill would have no idea what a chauvinist was. "I'll have you know I can do most things just about as well as anybody else, and some things a lot better than most people. I'm going, and that's all there is to it. And my brother won't go unless I go with him, isn't that right, Barnaby?"

Her twin hesitated a moment, remembering only too well the time when he had been held prisoner in this very castle by King Thorkin. Finally, he nodded. "I guess that's right, Lara," he said reluctantly, "but I really sort of wish you'd stay out here. Maybe I should just go in alone."

"No!" Lara was very firm, which helped hide from the others her fear of entering the castle. "Either we go together or not at all."

"And I'll go with them, in Barnaby's shirt pocket," Ergot declared. "That way the *topa* will work on me, too, without my having to eat any."

So that's the way it was decided. Ergot quickly got the remainder of his supply of *topa*, and Quill, along with the three Kewprums, went into hiding in the spot where the party had first encountered Ergot. From there they could see the west tower, where Barnaby said the secret room was located. If things got bad, they could make a rescue attempt at one of the tower windows. Quill even let Barnaby take his dagger — also his three-holed whistle, with which to signal for help if need be.

The twins — with Ergot in Barnaby's pocket — very carefully approached the causeway leading to Castle Thorkin. Not until there was no further hiding place did they grasp each other's hands and then chew up and swallow all of the *topa* mushrooms. Within moments they became invisible.

"Be sure to keep a tight grip on my hand, Lara," Barnaby said as they left their hiding place and walked out onto the causeway. "We don't dare get separated or we'd have a hard time finding each other again."

Lara tightened her grip and nodded, but then realizing her brother couldn't see her nod, murmured, "Okay, Barnaby. You hold tight, too."

"Good idea," Ergot rumbled softly.

There were a fair number of people — mostly Dwarfs, Dwirgs, Elves, Fauns and Tworps — crossing the causeway in both directions, and the line of guards flanking the road studied each passerby closely. The guards were mainly men, along with a few Dwarfs and Gnomes and a half-dozen Centaurs who clattered back and forth along the causeway on noisy hooves. There were also several of the fearsome crepuscular Krins, wearing orange-colored sunglasses to protect their eyes from the Mesmerian sunlight, their long whiplike tails coiled in readiness to strike and their wide, reptilian jaws bristling with sharklike teeth. Most of the guards had swords or spears, but some carried crossbows or longbows and their quivers bristled with a good supply of arrows. They seemed only too willing to use them. High above, hunched on the parapets and towers, were a dozen or more Vulpines. They looked sleepy and not particularly dangerous as they perched with their heads couched deeply in their shoulders, but both Barnaby and Lara knew only too well what terrible foes these huge greenish-black birds could be.

It was scary for the twins, walking right past the guards unseen. Even though invisible, they felt very exposed and helpless. One of the guards in particular — a mean-looking Dwirg — stared directly at the spot they were passing and his mouth opened in a big O. For an awful moment they thought that somehow he had discovered them and was preparing to give the alarm, but then they realized he was only yawning.

At the vast closed doors, which were the entrance to Castle Thorkin, they waited impatiently until a squad of Centaurs opened them to file through, and the three invisible intruders slipped inside at the same time. The trailing Centaur closed the doors behind him with a heavy booming thud and then caught up with the others. In a little while the clattering of their hooves faded away in the distant marble-floored corridors.

"C'mon." Barnaby's whisper was barely audible to Lara and she responded to his tugging on her hand. They moved quietly down a long corridor, staying close to the wall and moving with care around the many statues on pedestals. It was a corridor with which Barnaby was very familiar — the same one he had been brought down as a prisoner to the Great Hall, to face King Thorkin for the first time. Only this time he turned off into an intersecting corridor before reaching the Great Hall, and within another twenty or thirty yards was leading his sister up a curving flight of wide stone stairs. At the upper landing there were two doors, and he paused there a moment, as if trying to remember which was the correct one. A guard stood against the wall, leaning on his spear and half dozing.

It was a ticklish situation. Barnaby selected the door on the left and tripped the heavy iron latch as quietly as he could, nevertheless feeling his heart speed up when there was a faint metallic clank, and he also heard Lara suck in her breath. The guard remained unmoving, and the boy opened the door only enough to slip through. He pulled Lara inside after him and just as quietly closed the door. They found themselves in a large circular chamber with half a dozen doors at regular intervals. Almost directly across from them, standing partially hidden behind a statue of an upright bear, two guards — both of them Gnomes — were conversing in muted tones.

That they had now entered the base level of the tower was quickly apparent when they looked upward. It was as if they were in a giant silo, its roof hundreds of feet above them. Every fifty or sixty feet there was a narrow landing circling the inside wall.

"Do we have to go all the way up *there*, Barnaby?" Lara whispered in a squeaky voice.

Barnaby nodded and swallowed and held a finger to his lips. Then, realizing that she could see neither his nod nor his finger, he murmured, "Yes. Now hush and follow when I pull." He squeezed her hand reassuringly and gently pulled her along the wall, toward where another flight of stone steps, narrower than the first, spiraled upward from this landing to the next, about six stories above them.

They paused at the foot of the stairs and Barnaby leaned close to her and breathed a warning to keep very close to the wall and away from the unprotected edge. Then, towing her behind, he started up. Despite staying close to the wall, they were near enough to the edge that the farther up they went, circling and circling, the dizzier Lara became and the more she trembled. Barnaby felt this and three-fourths of the way up he paused long enough to put his free arm around her shoulders in a brief hug and breathe a word of encouragement.

"Get on with it!" rumbled the heavy whispered voice of Ergot from his breast pocket. "No time for lollygagging now. The *topa* may not last as long as we think. Go!"

They went on, reaching five more landings, passing more guards and five times more climbing long and ever-narrower flights of spiraling stone steps. The last flight was unguarded, but these steps were the worst — hardly more than a foot wide. They edged up them with great care, their backs sliding against the wall all the way, their grips on each other's hand tighter than ever. Lara helped ease her fear by closing her eyes, pretending the stairs were wider and then proceeding upward merely by the feel of the steps under her feet, the wall against her back and Barnaby's secure grip. Still, both she and Barnaby were breathing very heavily by the time they reached the final landing.

The landing was surprisingly large, but there was only one door here, a fairly heavy wood-plank barrier that was sealed with a heavy padlock. Lara expected Barnaby to lead her toward it, but instead he passed it by and then stopped, facing what appeared to be a blank stone wall — large blocks of stone separated here and there by smaller blocks.

"I'm going to release your hand for a minute, Lara," Barnaby whispered. "Stay exactly where you are. I'll be right back."

"Okay," she murmured back to him. She wondered what he was going to do and then it became clear, as she saw him stepping up close to the wall. She gasped.

"Barnaby! I can see you!"

7

A Towering Conflict

Barnaby swallowed audibly and looked down at himself, then back toward where Lara was standing.

"You're still invisible," he hissed. "How come I'm not?"

"I don't know!" Her whisper was a muted wail.

"It's elementary, my dear children," rumbled the voice of Ergot. "Barnaby is larger, his specific gravity is greater and therefore, due to his particular metabolism, the molecular viability of the *topa* has been more speedily consumed. Considering that he weighs approximately twelve pounds more than you and calculating the rate of reaction time he has undergone, into which we must divide your weight and specific gravity, it thereupon becomes clear that as of this moment you have approximately ten seconds of invisibility remaining . . . six . . . five . . . four . . . three . . . two . . . one . . . ."

An instant after his final word, Lara reappeared. Ergot popped his head up from Barnaby's pocket and grinned.

"Hi there!" His voice reverberated from the cold walls.

"Ergot, be quiet!" Barnaby warned in a low voice. "Do you want the guards to discover us?"

"Not to worry," the Shrood said reassuringly. "Taking into consideration the slight muffling quality of these stone walls, multiplied by the linear distance we have traveled, plus the altitude we have climbed above the last guards we passed, and adding to that the fact that they were engaging in conversation between themselves in subdued decibels, my voice, therefore, in a normal tone, will not be overheard. Nor will yours."

"Unless there's a guard standing around that we don't know about," Barnaby said grimly, but Lara noticed he was no longer whispering. He turned his attention back to the wall and studied it carefully, his eyes squinched together as he concentrated. Then he reached out and touched, in succession, four different blocks — three small and one large. After a moment he again touched one of the smaller ones he had touched before.

There was a heavy grumbling sound and a faint crack appeared in between the blocks.

"Did it!" Barnaby chortled, proud of himself for having remembered what Daw had told him so long ago.

The crack may have been there before, but the stone blocks had been so well fitted it had not been noticeable. Now the gap widened as a section of the wall pushed inward and the crack took the outline of a door. It groaned and grumbled more and slid back with excruciating slowness until it was an indentation of more than a foot.

Abruptly it came to a halt, still blocking the entry.

His sense of urgency growing, Barnaby tried again and again to make it open all the way by pressing the blocks in the correct sequence and then trying other combinations. It didn't move one iota.

"What are we going to do, Barnaby?" Lara asked, a quaver in her voice.

"I don't know!" He sounded as if he were not very far from tears himself.

"A process of elimination suggests," Ergot spoke up, his head protruding from the boy's pocket, "that disuse of the door, over a period of what may have been centuries, has allowed mildew, mosses, lichens, algae or other growths to become functionally established in the track of the door. The portal, sliding back in this manner, has undoubtedly scraped the material before it, causing it to accumulate and become binding in a confined space to the point where friction overcame rectilinear motion, causing a resumption of inertia and, therefore, cessation of normal operation."

"I think he means it's jammed," Lara said.

"Oh, that's just great! Here we are, visible again, and we can't get in. Now what?"

"Logic dictates that a solution is feasible," Ergot said. "In light of our previous conversations in the woods as we prepared to come here, it became evident that Lara at one point attended the Mesmerian School of Applied and Theoretical Magic, where she successfully completed the courses Magic One and Magic Two, though not yet Advanced Sorcery. Since one of the more elemental programs offered in the Magic One curriculum of that institute is portal control, and it is, in fact, a prerequisite for acceptance in Magic Two, it therefore stands to reason that Lara has acquired the necessary knowledge to serve our immediate needs in this capacity."

"I think that means . . ." Barnaby said slowly, and then the light dawned. "Lara, he's right! You can open it with your *Dehisce* spell. Go to it!"

Lara nodded, pointed a steady finger at the door and murmured, "*Dehisce.*"

The door did not move. The little girl was crestfallen.

"Louder, Lara," Barnaby said. "Make it a real command."

Again she pointed and this time she spoke considerably louder and with much more authority than before. "*Dehisce!*"

The great stone door groaned for a moment, but did not move. However, the padlock on the wooden door a short distance away popped open and swung pendulously from the latch.

"Again, Lara, again! Give it all the gusto you've got!"

She planted her feet more firmly, hunched her shoulders, lowered her head, pointed her finger ramrod straight at the door and frowned so deeply that her eyes were nearly closed.

"*DEHISCE!*" she cried.

A lot of things happened at once then:

. . . the great stone door gave a monstrous grinding groan and pushed the rest of the way inward, then slid smoothly out of sight into a hidden pocket of the wall.

. . . the wooden door that had become unlocked with Lara's second command now burst from its frame and flew out into the open air beyond the ledge, then plummeted toward the bottom.

. . . other doors on lower levels banged open in a variety of ways.

. . . all the other noises were punctuated by the loud crash of the door from their level finally hitting the bottom.

"Holy mackerel, Lara," Barnaby breathed wonderingly, "you're really *good!*"

Ergot, on the other hand, deduced that now was not the time for complimentary chatter. "I would call to your attention," he remarked, "that you have a maximum of two minutes and seventeen seconds remaining before you are confronted by some very angry guards."

The twins nodded and raced into the opening of the stone wall. The room they found was no wider than the door itself has been — hardly more than a large closet. An inch-wide slit in the outer wall, covered with bits of stained glass cemented into place, allowed a certain amount of dim light to filter into the room. The only furnishings were a large, sturdy, crudely made oak table and a slatted wooden chair. At the rear of the table, a fat stub of candle no more than an inch high squatted in the midst of a congealed puddle of melted tallow in a heavy bowl-type brass candle holder. In the middle of the table were two very large volumes bound in heavy leather, with rawhide ties holding the covers snugly shut. At the front of the table was another volume, just as large, lying open in about the middle. Bold writing and some strange symbolic drawings covered the exposed pages, but these were only dimly visible because of the layer of dust coating everything. The pages of this volume were held open by the weight of a short, silvery rod with a clear ball of flawless crystal about the size of a golf ball at one end and a loop of gold cord at the other. There was no doubt in their minds that this was the Wand.

Hypnotically, Lara picked it up. Her cheeks puffed out as she blew dust from it and then slipped the loop over her left wrist and pulled it snug. For just a moment the ball became rose red. She stiffened, much as if a small electrical charge had passed through her. Then, as the ball became clear again, she relaxed and smiled at Barnaby. "I'll take care of this," she told him.

Ergot, in the boy's shirt pocket, wrinkled his nose and sneezed as the puff of dust enveloped him, then commented dryly: "It doesn't take any great powers of logic to deduce that this room has not been used in a very *very* long time."

"Probably not since Warp was here, before the battle at the Twilandia Cliffs," Barnaby replied.

"Never mind that," Lara said excitedly. "Listen!"

From considerably below came the sound of many feet clattering up the steps, the clanking of armor and rattle of weapons, along with a babble of voices.

"Interesting," Ergot murmured. "We have precisely seventy-two seconds remaining before we are caught."

Without a word, Barnaby quickly leaned over the table and snatched up one of the two closed books. It was heavy enough to make him grunt with the effort. He turned and saying, "Can you carry this?" thrust it into Lara's arms. She nodded, even though she staggered slightly at the weight of it.

"I'll get the other one," he told her, "but we'll have to let the third one go. We can't carry all three."

Even as he spoke he grabbed up the second tied volume and they left the room in a staggering run, Barnaby

leading the way. Looking over the landing, he could see a dozen or more armed guards far below, racing up the steps. He dipped his head toward the open doorway where the wooden door had been and they ran inside. It was a storage room of some kind, crammed with dusty boxes and bales and bags with unknown contents.

At the moment, the twins had no time to be curious about what they contained. Their attention was centered on a high narrow window opening in the thick stone wall, though there was no glass or framework. It was wide enough for them to squeeze through if need be, but Barnaby gulped when he leaned over and looked out: There was a sheer drop of some three hundred feet to the jagged rocks below — rocks washed at their edges by the lapping waves of Green Lake.

Barnaby pulled back and plopped his book onto the

window ledge and dug a hand into his trousers pocket. It emerged with Quill's whistle. He leaped onto the ledge, stepped over the books — Lara had placed hers on top of his — and leaned out as far as he could. Well below and to his left was the forested mountain slope on which Quill and the Kewprums were hiding.

Ergot, peeking down out of the boy's pocket, kept saying, "Oh, my . . . Oh, my . . . Oh, my . . ."

Holding on as best he could with his left hand, Barnaby put the whistle to his lips with his free hand and blew three shrill blasts as he had seen Quill do. Then he repeated it. He was just preparing to blow it a third time when his grip slipped. In throwing out his arms to keep from falling out, he dropped the whistle. It hit the ledge at his feet, bounced into the air and fell out of sight.

Barnaby groaned.

An instant later he breathed a deep sigh of relief as he saw Kite, Kestra and Phalco rising above the trees. Quill was riding on the back of Kite, in the lead, but they were much farther away than Barnaby had thought they would be and he knew they could not reach them before the guards did. The situation became even worse when several of the voracious Vulpines hurled themselves into flight off the parapets, shrieking harsh alarms that would bring reinforcements.

Lara had not been idle while her brother was so engaged. She had raced back to the landing and looked down. The guards were no more than thirty or forty feet below and coming fast, so it was vitally important to close the heavy stone door of the secret room: She and Barnaby might not have been able to take the third book of the *Secret Volumes of Warp* themselves, but they couldn't afford to have it fall into the hands of the enemy.

Earlier, a tremendous reaction had occurred at her *Dehisce* command, due to the energy she had put into invoking it, but that was nothing compared to the urgency and strength she now poured into her delivery of the spell for door-closing.

"OCCLUDA!"

Within one second, the massive stone door thundered closed, sealing itself as invisibly as it had been when they first saw it. But her desperate invoking of the spell had much more far-reaching effects. All the doors that had opened at the Spell of *Dehisce* now slammed shut with fantastic force, the racket reverberating throughout Castle Thorkin. And at the same time, the door that had burst off this tower storage room and now lay on the stone floor far below, lifted and whistled upward, becoming a dangerous projectile.

Lara saw it coming and had only enough time to fall backwards into the room. Spinning through the air, the heavy plank door, now badly splintered in several places from its initial fall, slammed itself back into place. The fit was no longer secure, because much of the frame had blown out when the door went. But the door wedged itself securely enough to give those inside some additional precious seconds before the guards could break in — guards who had just this moment reached the landing.

Outside the window, matters had become hectic. While Kestra and Phalco hovered close by to pick up Lara and Barnaby, Kite — with Quill on his back — kept the Vulpines away. The huge, snaggle-beaked birds were much larger and better armed than Kite, but they were also more ponderous in flight, unable to maneuver with such consummate skill and grace as the Kewprum leader. He flew circles around them, throwing them off balance and, at least temporarily, keeping them away. And all the while, his white beard trailing behind him in the wind, Quill clung to Kite's neck, roaring with laughter.

Barnaby leaped back into the room to help Lara to her feet, then up onto the window ledge. Since there was no outer ledge on which the Kewprums could perch to pick them up, there was no way for the twins to get onto the backs of the birds, to say nothing of simultaneously carrying away the two precious *Secret Volumes of Warp*. The long, flapping wings of the Kewprums forced them to stay quite a few feet away from the tower wall.

The sudden crashing of battle-axes against the splintered storage room door became a crescendo above the surrounding din.

"Taking into consideration the present state of the door and remaining density of the planking," Ergot shouted from Barnaby's pocket, "and the velocity of the axes, multiplied by the weight of the axe heads, I would say we have fifteen seconds maximum before they break in."

The color drained from Barnaby's face. His hand went to his belt and he withdrew the dagger Quill had given him.

"It's no use!" Lara wailed. Tears were dribbling from her eyes as she stood close to him on the window ledge. "It's all over. We've lost!"

8

Flight

"WE'RE *not* LOST!" Barnaby shouted. "We'll get out of this — we *will!*"

"While we still have a second or so of grace," the deep voice of Ergot rumbled, "may I suggest, Lara, that you invoke your initial spell again?"

Immediately Lara nodded and pointed a quaking finger at the door.

"*Dehisce!*" she cried.

Once again the door blew outward with a terrific clatter and splintering of wood. The noise became louder as the door bowled over the six or seven guards who were on the other side and within an axe-stroke of breaking in. The broken door — along with the flailing, armor-clad guards — plunged off the ledge into space. Weapons flew spinning from their hands and their terrified, dwindling shrieks were suddenly cut short far below. There were still more guards on the steps, but now they hesitated, fearful of encountering the same stunning power.

Beside Lara on the ledge, Barnaby picked up both of the cumbersome volumes with an effort and held them up for Quill to see as he flashed past on Kite. At once the Dwarf leaned forward and said something to his feathered mount. Kite banked sharply and swept back, tilting so that one wing was up and the other down and the feathers of his underside were almost brushing the tower. As he arrowed past the window, his talons shot out and snatched the volumes from the boy's hand in a sure grip.

Taking this cue from their leader, Kestra and their nephew, Phalco, sped toward the window in the same way. Kestra got there first and adroitly plucked Lara from the ledge, the hooked beak snapping closed with amazing precision over the blousy back of her dress, while never touching her skin. The Wand, dangling from Lara's left wrist, glinted in the Mesmerian sunlight.

Phalco snatched up Barnaby in the same way, just at the instant that a dozen of Krumpp's guards rushed into the room brandishing their weapons. The Kewprum had closed his beak over the back of Barnaby's belt and now the boy hung doubled over, head and feet nearly meeting. In this position, his shirt pocket was upside down

and the little Shrood was now hanging grimly from the buttonhole.

"I would say," Ergot commented, with commendable calmness under the circumstances, "that we are at this moment at an altitude of three hundred feet. Should I fall, my rate of drop would be thirty-two feet per second per second. Therefore, by the time I hid the ground — which would be roughly four point two seconds — my terminal velocity would be one hundred thirty-eight point fifty-six feet per second, which comes to ninety-two point seven miles per hour. Chances for survival would be decidedly slim."

"Don't worry, Ergot," Barnaby reassured him, "you're not going to fall. We've gotten away from Castle Thorkin and we're safe now."

Unfortunately, Barnaby's assessment of their situation was premature. Ten voracious Vulpines were still pursuing them. Had the Kewprums been entirely unencumbered, they probably could have eluded these enemies with ease. But Kestra was burdened with Lara dangling from her beak, Phalco was burdened with Barnaby dangling from his beak and Ergot dangling from Barnaby's pocket, and Kite not only had Quill on his back, but the heavy *Secret Volumes of Warp* clenched in his talons.

Despite his load, Kite became a fearsome aggressor. He dived and whirled and looped, circled the enemy Vulpines with almost blinding speed and tore at each of the bigger birds with his beak as he passed. The giant bronze-colored birds were stubborn and certainly rather dim-witted, but even they finally realized they had met their match in Kite. One by one they veered off and winged wearily back toward Castle Thorkin, their wings and backs severely gouged by Kite's punishing beak.

Finally, only three of the Vulpines remained and now, seeing that Phalco was the youngest and least skilled in maneuvering while carrying a person in his beak, they concentrated their attack on him. While two kept him busy from the front, the third swept in at a screaming dive from the rear. Phalco spotted him at the last moment and tried to spin away, but he was too late. The multitoothed jaws of the great bird closed on one of his wings. There was a burst of beautiful copper feathers and a shriek from Phalco as a great gash appeared in his wing. He began losing altitude immediately.

Kestra, who was closest at that moment, instantly swept in and used her strong talons to pluck Barnaby by the scruff of his shirt — along with the still grimly hanging-on Ergot — from Phalco's beak, giving him a better opportunity to defend himself. It was too late. The wound in the younger Kewprum's wing was so severe that he continued spiraling downward. Like wild dogs closing in for the kill, the three Vulpines converged on him, ripping and tearing. Another cloud of coppery feathers burst free and suddenly Phalco was no longer spiraling down in a sort of helpless glide; he was tumbling end over end in a dead fall.

Too far above to help, Kestra and Kite shrieked with despair as their nephew fell. He hit the water of Green Lake with a loud splash and disappeared beneath the surface. Screaming triumphantly, the three cowardly Vulpines winged away at top speed toward Castle Thorkin, afraid to risk any further attack on Kite and Kestra.

The two remaining Kewprums set their wings and dived, not leveling off until they were scant feet above the choppy surface of the lake where Phalco had vanished. For a long while they circled, but though they saw some of their nephew's feathers floating on the surface, he did not reappear. At last Kite spoke softly to Kestra and the two ended their search and flapped sadly northward.

In the short time they had known him, the twins had grown very fond of Phalco. They were stricken with anguish that he was gone forever and there were no words of solace they could speak to Kite and Kestra that were adequate to their grief. Now safely back in Barnaby's pocket, even Ergot — who had seemed never at a loss for something to say — had no suitable words to speak. The party had successfully completed their very hazardous mission, but there was no joy in their hearts.

Phalco was gone.

They would never forget Phalco.

No one spoke much after that.

They flew northward in strained silence for hours, occasionally making wide circles to make sure they were not being followed. After leaving Green Lake far behind them, one brief stop was made, merely to readjust their loads. Kite, the strongest, took Barnaby, along with Ergot, on his back behind Quill. He also carried one of the heavy volumes in one set of talons, leaving his beak and the other foot free for action, should they be attacked again. Lara remained on Kestra's back and Kestra carried the other volume in one foot, leaving her as prepared for action, if necessary, as Kite. Then they took off again and continued flying in silence for a long while, northward across Rubiglen. Finally, following Quill's directions, they landed in the western foothills of the Ruby Mountains and found accommodations with two Dwarf friends of his — a jolly young married couple, Skaz and Ursha.

"Crobbity! Crobbity!" Skaz and Ursha cried, overjoyed at seeing Quill again. They welcomed his companions warmly and invited the six travelers into their home — an underground house they had built themselves beneath the roots of a gigantic gnarled tree. It was a surprisingly spacious and homey dwelling. While Ursha quickly went into a flurry of activity, cooking them a fine meal, Skaz got them settled in pleasant, individual rooms. The couple saw that their guests were weary and very sad about something, but they didn't pry. Their dinner conversation was light and as soon as the meal was finished, Skaz and Ursha insisted that their guests go to bed and get a good rest. Which is exactly what they did. The accommodations were wonderfully comfortable, but none of the six was thinking about comfort; the memory of Phalco was still a painful wound in the heart of each.

When they arose, refreshed, Lara suggested — and everyone else agreed with the idea — that they hold a brief memorial service for the lost Kewprum. When it was concluded, Barnaby borrowed a mallet and chisel from Skaz and spent the rest of the day carving a marker in a large square signboard. They nailed it to a big tree in a pleasant little glen not far from the underground dwelling. It read:

In fond memory of

— P H A L C O —

who died heroically,
giving his life so that
others who follow might
have a better and
happier one

R. I. P.

*At any hour she might be found bent over the pages, reading them
by the glow of the oil lamp—studying, learning, memorizing—concentrating
far harder than she ever had for schoolwork (page 93).*

Before any of them could move, a series of fuzzy white strands like strong yarn burst from underneath the rim of each of the fungi they were sitting on, crisscrossing their legs and arms and bodies in an instant, anchoring them in their sitting positions (page 119).

Lara's Decision

"SADNESS," SAID KITE, as they gathered later in the parlor of the underground house, "is never pleasant. But there are times when it is all a person can feel."

"Yes," Kestra said, "especially when a loved one has been lost." She nodded slowly and, uncurling her pinion feathers with which she had been holding her teacup, she placed it in the saucer with a musical little clink. "Such times can make permanent scars on a person's heart."

"That's true," Kite agreed. "Yet, in its own way, sadness can be very important in one's life. Without it, how could we ever truly experience happiness? Without it, how could we know when things were better?"

They were quiet for a short while, lost in their own

thoughts. Then Quill, who had been absently stroking his beard, cleared his throat and spoke softly. "Yes, while not pleasant, there is something to be said for sadness. Very often the grief we suffer can motivate us to do things that we would not be inclined to do if we were happy. Our present situation is a good example; our sadness at Mag Namodder's imprisonment and peril has inspired us to try to rescue her, because we know that if we are successful, it will restore happiness to us and to all of Mesmeria."

"That was what Phalco gave his life for," Kestra murmured, "and we would be failing him and ourselves and the people of Mesmeria if we were to let our grief and despair at losing him discourage us in our mission."

"I could not agree more," Kite said. "We must carry on with our efforts, not only to save Mag Namodder if we possibly can, but so that the loss of Phalco is not without meaning. Phalco would have been the first to urge us to carry on."

It was in this way that they were able to put the good memories of Phalco away for the present, in a very special place in their hearts, and return to the matter at hand.

The Wand had caused a definite change in Lara. With a soft cloth provided by their hostess, she had wiped away all lingering dust on the implement, murmuring more to herself than to the others as she inspected it, "Oh, I just love this! It's so . . . so . . . Oh, I *love* it!" Al-

though the golden cord was still looped firmly over her wrist, she gripped the silvery shaft in her hand and a glow came into her cheeks and her eyes sparkled. She looked somehow older and wiser; self-assured and serene.

By unspoken agreement, Ergot had now become one of them, as much concerned with the plan to rescue Mag Namodder as any of the others. Quill, in private, told the other five members of their party that he thought Skaz and Ursha should be informed of their mission and what had happened at Castle Thorkin. They all agreed and, not unexpectedly, the two Dwarfs were very excited, offering their help in any way possible.

Ursha had uncommonly pretty features. She was a robust woman, an inch shorter than Skaz, who was three feet tall. Her voice was lilting and clear-toned and she almost always sang as she worked. She especially enjoyed cooking and was forever concocting sumptuous meals that pleased everyone. Many years ago she had been a member of the Supreme Committee of Rubiglen, but she really preferred the simple life. Now she took great pride in simply being a homemaker and the wife of Skaz. She thought she might possibly like to have children later on, but not yet; there was plenty of time for that. After all, she and Skaz could still be considered newlyweds, having been married only thirty-five years. She thought that perhaps, after they'd been married for about a century, they might consider raising a family.

Skaz was a rosy-cheeked, pipe-smoking individual. Unlike most of the Dwarfs, he was uncommonly thin and his head was covered with a bushy growth of curly black hair. His ears were sharply pointed at top and bottom. Years ago, before Krumpp had conquered Mesmeria, Skaz had worked in the ruby mines. Now he was a prospector and delighted in showing these guests his fine collection of cut and uncut rubies, emeralds and diamonds. He was an avid reader with a fine little library and he was, above all, intelligent. In fact, he and Ergot immediately struck up a close friendship and were soon spending many hours together discussing history and science and philosophy and other subjects in which they were both interested.

After hearing the story of the events that had brought

Quill and his friends here, Skaz suggested that it might be wise to inform certain former leaders of Mesmeria of their plans. These leaders, he said, were in hiding from Krumpp, who would have them executed should he find them. Skaz knew how to reach them and he was confident they would be most anxious to help in any way possible. They agreed, although Ergot was a little dubious of the value of letting too many people see them.

"We still have an important mission to accomplish," he said, "and any help would be welcome, but for the moment the key to rescuing Mag Namodder and the others seems most likely to be something we might find in the two *Secret Volumes of Warp* we took from Castle Thorkin."

"That's very probably exactly right, Ergot," Quill said, bowing to the Shrood's logic. "It should be our first priority to see what help the books may be to us."

Thereupon, everyone assembled in Skaz's cozy little library, gathering curiously around the table upon which rested the huge *Secret Volumes of Warp*. Under the warm yellow light of the oil lamp they discovered that the leather bindings had been gouged a bit from where the Kewprums' talons had gripped them — for which Kite and Kestra apologized profusely — but otherwise they were intact.

They were eager to see what was written in the fabled books, but their interest did not last long. There was no title page; the first page of the book marked *Volume I* carried only a decidedly sobering warning. To begin with, for all but Lara, that warning was the only clearly understandable writing in the book; the remainder was a peculiar mixture of weird symbols, hieroglyphic writing and a strange language that only *she* seemed capable of deciphering to a limited degree. The warning was penned in a beautiful and elaborate script, brief and to the point:

BEWARE
Ye Who Would Enter Here
+ + + * * * + + +
Look not lightly on these
Spells
lest their awesome
Power
reverse itself and
destroy the unknowing fools
who might dare to invoke them.
+ * +

Having read that initial page, Skaz and Ursha, as well as the Kewprums, became frightened; they not only would not even come near the books again, they were disinclined to enter the room where the volumes were resting. Quill and Ergot glanced nervously at a few pages beyond that. Quill finally admitted that, although he could make out a little of the writing, he too was afraid to go further. Therefore, he also avoided entering the library where Lara was studying them. Ergot lasted a few pages beyond that, but he finally reasoned that he had no business looking at such things and left the room. Barnaby was uneasy, though not really afraid, and he glanced through both volumes at random before finally giving up, mainly because he simply could not understand any of it.

For his sister, it was another matter.

In the weeks that followed, Lara hardly knew what the others were doing. She became so totally absorbed in studying the *Secret Volumes of Warp* that she scarcely took time to eat or sleep. Ursha brought food to her at regular intervals, and Lara ate and drank mechanically. Occasionally after reading a particular passage, she would hold the Wand in both hands and examine it closely, but she never disengaged the cord that attached it to her wrist. At any hour she might be found bent over the pages, reading them by the glow of the oil lamp — studying, learning, memorizing — concentrating far harder than she ever had for schoolwork. At those infrequent times when exhaustion forced her to stop and throw herself down on the cot that had been brought into the room for her, she slept fitfully, no more than a few hours at a time. As she slept she gripped the Wand and, on occasion, the clear ball of crystal on its end would briefly become red or blue or yellow. Several times Lara moaned or cried out in her sleep, which would awaken her and she would immediately return to her study of the *Secret Volumes of Warp*. Ursha was becoming concerned at the way Lara was driving herself.

So intense was Lara's concentration on the books, she was unaware that Quill, Skaz and Barnaby, with Ergot in his pocket, flew off on the Kewprums twice — once back to Twilandia for a few days and once on a more extensive and definitely more hazardous mission to visit the hidden communities throughout Mesmeria, not only here in the country of Rubiglen, but also in the more distant countries of Selerdor and Mellafar and even Verdancia.

At last, one day she emerged, drawn and pale, from the library. She joined the others just in time for tea and smiled at them weakly.

"I've finished," she told them, "at least for now."

"You learned all the spells?" Barnaby asked eagerly.

She shook her head and laughed tiredly. "No, I'm afraid not. It would take years of study to learn all that is in those books, but I may have learned enough to help us some. I hope so, because we don't have much time."

"What do you mean, Lara?" Quill asked, his brow furrowed with sudden concern.

"Logic dictates what she means," Ergot spoke up from Barnaby's pocket.

"Even if it does," Barnaby said a little sharply, before Egot could go on, "it should be up to Lara to tell us in her own way."

Ergot hung his head and nodded. "Right," he said. "Absolutely right. I've just got to learn to stop answering other people's questions. Sorry."

But Lara did not answer Quill's question at once; instead she asked him one in return. "How long ago, exactly, was Mag Namodder captured? What I need to know is, how long has she been held prisoner in Melanistica?"

"Well, she was captured somewhat over seven hundred and forty-nine years ago. Come to think of it, I guess it's much closer to seven hundred and fifty years, now. So far as we know, she was shipped off to the island dungeon in Melanistica within a couple of days after that."

Lara was not completely satisfied with the answer. "How *close* to seven hundred and fifty years ago? Can you remember? It's *very* important, Quill."

The Dwarf stroked his beard for a moment, then shook his head and shrugged. "I don't recall *exactly*, but . . ."

"I do!" interjected Skaz. "It was just two days before Rubiglen's biggest holiday, the Festival of the Satyrs."

"And how near is that?"

"Why, it's . . . let's see . . . this is the tenth of Orben and the festival is on the fourth of Ennaben. That means Krumpp captured Mag Namodder on Ennaben second."

Lara persisted. "How many days away is Ennaben second?"

"Well, the month of Orben has twenty-two days, so it's fourteen days from now."

The little bit of color still in Lara's face drained away.

"Lara, what's the matter?" It was Barnaby.

"Are you ill, dear?" asked Ursha worriedly, rising and coming quickly to the girl's side.

Lara shook her head and tried to smile, but failed. When at last she spoke, her words were barely audible and they sent a chill through all who were there.

"I'm afraid Mag Namodder is in worse peril than any of you realize. Because of the powers that a sorcerer has, I know now that Mag Namodder has not been killed by Krumpp. I cannot put into terms that would make sense to you why I know this to be true. For the time being, trust me that it is. The more important thing is that she is going into a period of extreme jeopardy right now. If we do not find her, rescue her and have her back in Mesmeria within fourteen days, she will die."

10

Mag Namodder's Peril

It was Barnaby who found his voice first after Lara's frightening pronouncement. What he said aloud was what all the others were thinking.

"What do you mean, Lara? How could something like that be?"

Lara shook her head sadly. "I wish I were wrong, but I'm afraid I'm not. The power of sorcery can be very great, but it also has certain limitations. It needs . . ." she paused, searching for the correct words, then went on, ". . . I can't say it in the way the books did, but what it means is that in order for someone to do magic, he has to have . . . to have . . . well, it's like having a battery charged to make it keep doing what it's supposed to do. That's not exactly how the *Secret Volumes of Warp* say it, but that's pretty close to what it means."

"You mean Mag Namodder's battery is run down?" Barnaby asked.

Lara nodded, but to the others the explanation was meaningless, since no one in Mesmeria had ever harnessed electric power.

"What's a battery?" Ergot asked, fascinated by the introduction of something into the conversation that he'd never heard about.

"And how do you make it run up if it is run down?" asked Kite.

"I don't understand any of it," said Kestra, shaking her head.

"I'll try to make it clear," Lara told them. "A battery is like a sort of storage container, and what it stores is power. But it only *stores* it; it can't create it. So when power is used from a battery, it has to be put back. That's called recharging. If it isn't put back, pretty soon you wind up with a dead battery."

She saw that everyone but Barnaby was frowning, not really grasping the idea, and so she tried to simplify the explanation.

"Mag Namodder has magical powers," she said. "They are powers for good, just as there are also magical powers for evil, such as the powers King Krumpp is said to have. Then there are neutral magical powers, which are neither good nor bad . . . they're just there. A good sorcerer, like Mag Namodder, can cast spells that come from a good power source, but not those that come from an evil power source. And an evil sorcerer, like Krumpp, casts spells from an evil power source but not from a good power source. And then there is some overlapping, because both of them can use the same neutral spells."

"Like the Spell of *Dehisce* for opening doors?" Barnaby put in.

"And the Spell of *Occluda* for closing them?" Quill added.

"Yes," Lara said. "Those are neutral spells, but there are others — and I dare not mention their names unless they are to be invoked — that are strictly for good or evil use."

"Logical," Ergot said. "Quite logical."

Ursha shook her head. "But what," she asked, "has all this to do with Mag Namodder?"

"Just this," Lara said. "A good sorcerer, such as Mag Namodder, gets her original power source from the rays of the Mesmerian sun. So long as she gets exposed to the sun occasionally, her power remains at its peak. And since Mesmeria has no night, this means every time she goes outside, her power is recharged."

"All right," Skaz put in, "I can undersand that, but what is the source of power for an evil sorcerer such as Krumpp?"

"I'm not yet entirely sure of that," Lara replied, "although I have an idea. But there isn't time to go into that right now. The important thing is the peril that Mag Namodder is in. According to the *Secret Volumes of Warp*, if a sorcerer of good magic is kept in darkness for any length of time, whatever power she has to cast her spells begins to fade. The longer she is kept in darkness, the more the power source is drained. Even if Krumpp had not originally put her under a spell that robbed her of ability to cast her own spells, eventually the darkness of her dungeon would have done the same thing."

"Then all of her power is gone?" Quill asked with a stricken expression.

"Can she never get it back?" Ursha was very upset.

"I suspect it's even worse than that," the tiny Shrood spoke up to no one in particular, his deep voice filling the room.

"You're right, Ergot," Lara said softly. Her voice shook a little and it was obvious she was having a difficult time keeping her composure. "You see, there is more to invoking spells than just a draining of power. Any person can learn elementary magic and even some of the fundamentals of sorcery. But at a certain stage of advancement, the person has to make a decision: He or she must decide whether or not to go into higher levels of sorcery and, at the same time, the decision must be either for good or for evil. It cannot be both. The only alternative is to turn back entirely and not enter high-level sorcery at all. And once a decision is made — for good or for evil or for turning back — it cannot be changed."

Barnaby's eyes widened. "Lara," he gasped, "you didn't!"

She nodded. "I did, Barnaby. I am now a good sorcerer on Level One of the High Plane. I can never change that. But it is only the barest of beginnings; the level I am on is the lowest true sorcerer level. There are ten levels of sorcery in the High Plane that I have to master before I am eligible for the Higher Plane, and twenty more in that before I can reach the Highest Plane. How far I might go in that, I have no idea." She gave a short, ironic laugh that made them all very uneasy. "Actually," she went on, "I'll need years and years of experience just to become eligible for advancement to the Higher Plane."

Barnaby was still aghast at Lara's having made such a decision. "You can't just back out if you want to?" he asked worriedly.

She smiled at him and shook her head. "Not only can't," she explained, "but wouldn't want to. It's the most wonderful thing that's ever happened to me. I have to admit that it took a lot of thinking to make the decision. When I did, and finally crossed the line — with no possibility of ever turning back — it was like taking a beating with a rubber baseball bat for a few days. If it hadn't been for having the Wand, I don't think I could have done it. You see," she held up the Wand for all to see, "*this* may be as important as the three volumes . . . maybe even *more* important. But enough about that for now."

Her gaze swung to Quill and Ursha, who were sitting on a sofa with Skaz. "In answer to your questions, yes, Mag Namodder's power is all gone. I don't know yet, Ursha, if she'll ever get it back. What's most important is what I *do* know: A sorcerer, whether for good or evil, cannot stay away from the power source indefinitely. Once a certain point is reached — and it is a clearly defined point — that sorcerer will die."

Ursha became pale. "And that point is . . . ?"

"Obviously, seven hundred and fifty years," Ergot spoke up. He glanced at Lara apologetically and closed his mouth with a little snap.

Lara nodded sadly. "Yes, that's right. *Exactly* seven hundred and fifty years. So I'll repeat what I said earlier: If we don't find Mag Namodder, rescue her somehow and have her back here in Mesmeria within fourteen days, she will die."

An uncomfortable silence fell over the little group, which was finally broken when Barnaby cleared his throat self-consciously and spoke up.

"Then we have no time to waste. We won't even have time to raise a rescue party from among the people we've contacted in the underground communities. We have to start our search immediately — today!"

"Within hours, if possible," Quill said. He turned to

Ursha. "Can you prepare some food supplies for us? Enough to last the six of us for fourteen days?"

"Of course," Ursha replied without hesitation.

Quill turned to face Skaz. "And can you, my friend, supply any sort of weapons for Barnaby and Lara and me? Also for Ergot, Kite and Kestra? All we have is one short dagger." He patted the weapon in his belt, which Barnaby had returned to him some time ago.

"Kestra and I don't need weapons," Kite put in quickly. "Ours are built in."

"Nor do I," Lara said quietly. She knew she didn't need to explain why not; the Wand in her grasp was almost a living presence.

"You wouldn't have anything small enough for me," Ergot said, adding sadly, "No one ever thinks of the little guy when they design things."

"Well, I'd sure like *something* if we're going into Darkland," Barnaby said. "And you ought to have a better weapon than that dagger, Quill."

"You're right." The white-bearded Dwarf nodded.

"I'll get weapons for the three of us, then," Skaz said.

Ursha looked at her husband in a frightened way and Quill put up a hand and spoke. "No, my friend, you're not going."

"But you're going to need all the help you can get!" Skaz objected.

"It would be nice if we had more help," Quill admitted, "but your place is here, Skaz, with Ursha. For several good reasons. We very well may need your assistance and your home as a headquarters if we get back. We'll be moving as fast as we can, and the loads that Kite and Kestra will have to carry just to transport us and our supplies, to say nothing of possibly having to fight off attackers at the same time, will make it difficult as it is. Finally, your place is here with Ursha so you can —"

He broke off abruptly as there came an urgent knocking on the front door. They looked at one another and Skaz shook his head.

"I'm not expecting anyone," he said. "I can't imagine who it is."

Lara, gazing raptly at the crystal knob on the Wand, lifted her eyes and smiled faintly. "The visitor is no one to fear," she said quietly, "though he is very troubled."

Skaz nodded uncertainly and moved toward the door. Quill limped along with him.

"It's reasonable to assume that whoever it is," Ergot said, "has come as a direct result of our visits to the underground communities. I trust everyone remembers that I warned of the probable results should we see too many people. But then, who takes the warning of a little person seriously? Nobody, that's who. That's the price you pay for being little."

They ignored his comments, all eyes on Skaz and Quill.

"Who's there?" Skaz called, stopping at the door.

"Skaz!" came an excited voice from outside. "It's Groad. I have some important news. Let me in!"

"He's a friend of mine," Skaz murmured. "It's all right." Nevertheless, as Skaz opened the door, Quill unsheathed his dagger and stood to one side, prepared for almost anything.

Groad turned out to be a Centaur, large and powerful. The upper part of his body was the torso, head and arms of a man, the chest heaving as he gasped for breath; but the lower part was the body of a large, sleek horse, its flanks presently soaked with perspiration. He ducked low to enter the doorway, just managing to squeeze in, and softly clumped into the middle of the room on remarkably gentle hooves.

"Crobbity, Skaz. I've come a long way — all the way from Green Lake in three days. I've hardly stopped. I left there the day after you visited us with these two." He indicated Barnaby and Quill with a wave of his hand.

The twins looked at one another. Even though they had been carried on the backs of the swift-flying Kewprums, it had taken them quite a few hours to get here from Verdancia's Green Lake when they fled from Castle Thorkin. For Groad to have made the same journey in only three days by running cross-country, over streams and mountain ranges, was quite an accomplishment.

"Crobbity, Groad," Skaz responded, then added quickly, "What's wrong?" In his haste and concern he neglected to introduce the Centaur to the others, but no one minded.

"Take a look at this," the Centaur said, undoing the flap of the pouch he carried over one shoulder and reaching inside. He extracted a rolled-up paper and handed it to Skaz. "They've been posted all over Verdancia and Rubiglen. Everywhere else in Mesmeria, too, so far as I know."

Skaz unrolled the paper and everyone crowded around to see. It was a Royal Proclamation by King Krumpp:

* NOTICE * NOTICE * NOTICE *

By Order of His Royal Highness

K   R   U   M   P   P

Benevolent Protector of All Mesmeria

***

HEAR YE:

Intruders have entered our midst and are causing great turmoil in the minds of the good people here living. They have defiled the Royal Castle Thorkin through illegal entry, theft, and murder of His Majesty's guards. Six perpetrators were involved in this incident, one of whom was caught and executed for his crime. The other five remain at large, including two Kewprums of as yet unknown identity; a fugitive Dwarf tentatively identified as Quill, who is believed to have been hiding in Twilandia until recently; and a witch and warlock disguised as small children, but possessing very dangerous magical powers.

REWARD:

His Benevolent Majesty herewith offers very rich rewards and a place in his Royal Court to any person(s) capturing or killing, or assisting in the capture or death, of any of the perpetrators. Similar rewards will be made for the return of the property stolen by these thieves. Since it would benefit King Krumpp to be able to personally question these criminals, a much greater reward will be made for bringing them in alive.

WARNING:

Any person suspected of aiding or abetting these criminals shall be put in irons and incarcerated in the Castle Thorkin dungeons until the return of his Benevolent Royal Majesty from Black Castle in Bluggia, at which time those so incarcerated will be subjected to intensive questioning by whatever means required for the extraction of information and at whatever risk may be involved to the health or life of the person(s) being questioned.

Any person(s) in His Benevolent Royal Majesty's Realm, including any of its protectorates or occupied provinces, who is found actually aiding or in any manner abetting these criminals, shall, without any exception, be summarily executed.

KRUMPP

***

"I'm a witch, disguised as a small child?" said Lara, a faintly amused smile on her lips.

"And I'm a warlock?" said Barnaby, grinning.

"And we're all criminals with a price on our heads!" added Kite.

"As usual," Ergot complained in a deep growl, "the little guy is totally ignored. What's the use of being a hero if no one even knows you were there?"

It was Quill, however, who detected the more important message for them in the document. "Well," he said, "at least we know now where to begin our search for Mag Namodder."

"We do?" questioned Kite.

"Where?" asked Kestra.

"That's obvious," Ergot interjected, not caring that the questions had been directed to Quill. "The Black Castle of Bluggia. Logic suggests that if we go there, we'll find more than just King Krumpp."

11

Flight into Darkness

SKAZ WORE A sad expression and Ursha was openly weeping when the six said their farewells and set out an hour or so later on their dangerous mission toward the unknown darkness of Melanistica. Skaz very solemnly shook the hands of Quill and Ergot and the twins, while Ursha kissed each in turn, and then they both embraced the two Kewprums. No one put it into words, but the feeling was strong that they'd never see one another again.

Kite was in the lead, carrying Quill and Barnaby on his back. The boy, with Ergot once again in his shirt pocket, had a medium-sized sword given to him by Skaz, while the Dwarf was now armed with a short, broad-bladed sword in addition to his dagger. Kestra was fol-

lowing, carrying Lara on her back and, about her neck, a large pouch containing food supplied by Ursha for them all.

Lara had the Wand with her, but they had not brought the *Secret Volumes of Warp*; Lara had not wanted to leave them behind, but was fearful of taking them along, lest they fall into the hands of the enemy. So, while the others made preparations for the trip (except for Ergot, who was taking a nap in a flowerpot), Lara and Barnaby had taken the big books to a meadow only a short distance from Skaz and Ursha's house. There, Skaz had told her, they would find a large outcropping of rock that he called Green Cliff. And so they had — a sheer wall of solid gray-green rock jutting from the delicate lavender grasses. Lara had inspected it by placing her hands flat against the cool surface and rubbing it, then murmuring in a satisfied way. She had stepped back a dozen feet, pointed the Wand at the wall and said in a loud voice, "*Vuga!*"

At once a cleft had formed in the wall, opening slowly until a sort of globular pocket had been formed in the solid rock, about two feet deep and perhaps thirty inches in diameter. Then she and Barnaby placed the two large *Secret Volumes of Warp* into the center of the circular area. They stepped back, and Lara again pointed the Wand at the area.

"*Avuga!*"

The opening to the pocket in the rock closed as swiftly and securely as a camera lens. It sealed itself so invisibly there was no indication of anything being there, except for a two-inch-high block-letter *L* that looked as if it had been chiseled into the rock face by a passerby. The children had returned then and told no one how the volumes were hidden.

Now they were headed north and the miles swept by quickly beneath them as the Kewprums settled into a strong, steady pace which they could maintain for long periods without tiring. All of them were experiencing a sense of rising fear the farther they traveled. At first there were roads here and there, along with the ruins of villages, plus a few familiar landmarks. One of these was the eastern shore of Amethyst Lake. Daw City was on the far side of the lake and, though they were at a considerable altitude, Lara thought she could detect the big boulder that marked the entrance to the Twilandia tubes.

Soon there were no more roads or deserted villages and nothing looked at all familiar. The fields had become vast bramble patches and the woodlands were tangles of interlocking branches without any visible paths. It would have been very difficult traveling for anyone afoot.

"Where are we now, Quill?" Barnaby called.

The Dwarf turned and looked back at them, holding his beard down with one hand to keep it from blowing in his face. "We're about as far north as I've ever been," he said. "Close enough to the Dymzonian border that it's a dangerous area and few people ever come here. The Krins and Vulpines are known to make frequent raids here from their own country, so it's not a healthy place to be. I don't know exactly how far ahead the border is."

"Only a few minutes," spoke up Kite, setting his wings to glide down to a much lower altitude. "I've flown this area a number of times on militia patrol. I think you should know that we won't be flying too much longer. You can see it's not quite so bright out anymore."

That was true, although the others hadn't noticed it until he said so. The daylight had lost much of its intensity, and they saw that the sun was close to the southern horizon far behind them. The long, narrow east-west country of Dymzonia, they knew, was the border nation between Mesmeria and Melanistica — the former always bright from the Mesmerian sun, the latter always dark, with no sunlight at all. The southernmost portions of Dymzonia were in a state of perpetual twilight and the farther north one went, the darker this twilight became. At the northern border, leading into Melanistica, Dymzonia was almost wholly dark.

Now, as Kite leveled off and Kestra followed him just over the silhouetted treetops, he continued speaking.

"We'll have to land before we enter the region of full darkness or we're apt to have some serious problems. There could be taller forests ahead that we might run into, or even mountains. And," he added grimly, "stay on the alert now. Chances are we'll be encountering some Vulpines soon."

"What about Krins?" Barnaby asked.

"We won't have to worry about them," Kite replied, "until we're on the ground."

"We may not have to land until we want to, Kite," Lara said. "I've learned some spells that may help." With elbows far outstretched, she held the Wand upright in both hands and touched the ball to her forehead, murmuring two words.

"*Lumini! . . . Luxa!*"

They couldn't see that anything in particular had happened, but after ten or fifteen seconds she smiled and said, "Kite, I think it might be best if you let Kestra take the lead, with you following. She'll be glowing faintly, so that should be easy enough, but be sure to make the same maneuvers we make. Quill, wherever possible, you should continue to give general directions about which way you think we should go. Meanwhile, I'll try to think of something else that may help us."

Kite immediately fell in directly behind Kestra, matching her wingbeat for wingbeat, movement for movement. Dimming daylight turned to dusk and dusk to very dim twilight as they continued northward. Soon they were in total darkness and the only thing visible was a pale blue aura outlining Kestra, caused by the Spell of *Lumini*. For Kite, following, it was not difficult, since he only had to follow Kestra, but for Kestra, in the lead, there was nothing but darkness ahead. Fortunately, the Spell of *Luxa* allowed Lara to see with reasonable clarity about a hundred feet in all directions. Every now and again she would lean forward and say, "Curve left," or "Curve right," or "Climb a little higher," and Kestra would obey immediately, followed by Kite. Once, when Kestra responded a little late, the bird felt the branches of a tree barely brush her underside. Another near disaster came ten minutes later.

"Sharp left!" Lara cried urgently.

Kestra veered at once, but nevertheless felt the whoosh of air as her wingtips barely grazed the face of a towering cliff.

"My!" Lara said. "That was certainly a strange formation — a very narrow rock pushing way up into the air all by itself, like a big needle. That may turn out to be a good landmark for us. We'll call it Needle Rock, okay?"

"Since you saw it first," Quill said, "I think we should call it Lara's Needle."

Barnaby and Ergot and the Kewprums agreed that was a fine name and so it was settled, though Ergot was heard to grumble to himself, "If you can't see it, then it's not much of a landmark!"

At last Lara directed Kestra into a circular flight pattern and then to a landing. For all — except Lara, of course — this was a nerve-racking moment, since they could not see what they were landing on, nor even the ground until they touched it. As soon as the Kewprums landed, the aura outlining Kestra faded away, leaving the party in total darkness. For several moments after they ceased moving, their hearts — except Lara's — continued pounding rapidly. The surface under their feet had a peculiar soft feel with hardness beneath the softness.

"What is this place?" rumbled the Shrood's deep voice.

"It's a high ledge," Lara explained, "overlooking a place where two small rivers come together — one from the west and one from the north — to form a larger one that flows toward the east. I think it may be important that we name the rivers — and even this ledge, too — so that if we need to refer to them again, we'll know exactly what we're talking about."

"Good idea," Quill agreed. "But what kind of a ledge is this we're on? It feels very strange underfoot."

"It's rock covered with white moss and some most unusual-looking plants growing here. They look like toadstools. Anyway, I don't see any sign of danger, so it looks like a safe enough place for us to stop and have something to eat and to rest."

"And," put in Kite, "to discuss where we're going. We can't continue flying blind like this." Kestra agreed, stretching expansively and breathing a sigh of relief as she removed the heavy pouch from about her neck and placed it on the ground at her feet.

"I sure don't like this darkness," Barnaby complained. "It's scary." There was a touch of envy in what he said next: "Lara, now that you've got the Wand, can't you make it so all of us can see?"

"No, not yet," she replied. "There's an awful lot about spell-casting, with or without the Wand, that I still don't understand. I just wish there'd been more time to study the books. But there's one thing I *can* do that might make us all feel a little better."

They couldn't see what she was doing, but she held out the Wand in both hands about a foot over the ledge and softly murmured a single word.

"*Conflagra.*"

At once a dozen or more glowing sticks appeared on the white moss and in a moment a small fire — cheery, bright and completely smokeless — sprang into life, illuminating their immediate area, including quite a large number of peculiar low growths that seemed to be knee-high, triple-stemmed fungi. These giant mushrooms looked very much like three-legged stools and made ideal seats for the little party.

They rummaged about in the pouch and soon were dining on little sandwiches made from slices of *metta-metta* on thin round toasted wafers. *Metta-metta* was one of the principal foods of Mesmeria. It was a vegetable that looked to Lara and Barnaby something like an eggplant in size and shape, but tasted exactly like meat. The kind of meat it tasted like depended on its color: dark red tasted just like roast beef, dark blue like boiled ham, dark green was much like leg of lamb and dark brown had the taste of roast pork. Inside each *metta-metta* was a seed about the size of a Ping-Pong ball and the seed itself, in sections something like a tangerine, was crisp and juicy and tasted like a perfectly ripe Jonathan apple, making it a very nice dessert.

Stopping here was just like having a campfire picnic. The fire did much to dispel their lingering fear, and the food restored their energy and made them feel better. As they sat in a circle on the peculiar plants and ate, they discussed this location and decided on names for the rivers and ledge. The stream coming from the west was named the Kestra River, while that coming from the north was named Kite River. The larger river, formed by the confluence of these two streams and flowing eastward, they named the Phalco River. And, to Ergot's delight, Lara's suggestion was enthusiastically adopted that they name this place where they were resting Ergot's Ledge.

They also discussed how fortunate it was that they had not yet encountered any of the deadly crepuscular Krins or voracious Vulpines.

"Where do you think we are now?" Barnaby asked of no one in particular, brushing crumbs off his lap.

"Estimating our air speed as having been a constant of sixty miles per hour," Ergot spoke up, "and taking into consideration that it was essentially direct-line flight, we have come slightly over three hundred miles."

"That tells us how many miles we've flown," Barnaby pointed out, "but it certainly doesn't tell us where we *are*."

Ergot had no answer for that, so he simply stretched out on his back on the comfortable surface of the fungus, fingers interlocked behind his neck.

Lara swallowed the last bite of her *metta-metta* sandwich. "I'm pretty sure," she said, "that Lara's Needle was on the northern border of Dymzonia, or at least very close to it. That means we're now well inside the country of Bluggia. Of course," she admitted, "that still doesn't tell us exactly where we are."

It was Quill who, clearing his throat, asked the key question on everyone's mind: "Well, Lara, what do we do now? Since you're the only one who can see in this darkness, which way do we go now? How do we find the Black Castle?"

Lara opened her mouth to explain some of the powers of the Wand — how it magnified her own abilities and some other special attributes it had which might serve them in their search for Mag Namodder — but before she could say a word, a harsh, gravelly voice growled an answer to Quill's question from directly beneath her.

"You won't *have* to find Black Castle. That's where you're going, like it or not!"

Before any of them could move, a series of fuzzy white strands like strong yarn burst from underneath the rim of each of the fungi they were sitting on, crisscrossing their legs and arms and bodies in an instant, anchoring them in their sitting positions. In an instant, Lara — along with her Wand — was pinned as if she were covered by a fish net. Quill and Barnaby were in the same fix and though they tried to use their swords, they could not, because their arms were snugged tightly to their sides. Ergot, flat on his back, was crisscrossed by several of the strands and able to move only his head. Kite and Kestra tried to tear at the cords with their beaks and talons, but they were hopelessly pinned.

"*Do* something, Lara!" Barnaby yelled. "Help us!"

But Lara, looking down at the strands imprisoning her, seemed unable to do anything at all. She shook her head and replied in a frightened voice.

"I'm afraid they've got us, Barnaby."

12

Tripodians

"WHO ARE YOU?" demanded Quill, his bushy white brows drawn together in a scowl and his beard quivering with fury. "By what right have you tied us up like this?"

"Just like a Brightlander to start off asking a nonspecific question," grumbled the fungus-like creature who had spoken before and who had imprisoned Lara. "Who am I, personally? Or who are we, as a group? Or who are we as a race? Or who are we in the grand scheme of the infinite cosmos? Be specific!"

"Atta boy, Captain," said the one who was holding Quill. "You tell 'em!"

"Give 'em what for, Captain," gloated the one holding Barnaby.

"I'll second that!" chortled the one holding Kite.

"Me, too, Captain," giggled the one holding Ergot, "me, too!"

"Make 'em toe the line, Captain!" said the one holding Kestra. "Set 'em straight!"

This was followed by a chorus of voices, praising the Captain for his comment. By the light of the flickering fire, the prisoners could see a swarm of the odd fungus creatures moving in more closely. Their movement on the three stems was much like the movement of someone on crutches, where the outer supports were thrust forward first to a firm stance and then the center one comes forward as well. Soon the captives were surrounded by twenty or thirty of them.

Now that they were moving about as animated creatures, their features became more apparent. Large dark eyes — six to an individual — were set on the rim of the mushroomlike cap, two positioned forward, two pointing backward and one each on the sides. The eyes seemed to have neither whites nor irides, only large, deep pupils. They reminded Barnaby of the oversized dark eyes of the flying squirrel he had once had as a pet. However, the eyes of these creatures, when closed, were covered by eyelids that blended so well with the skin of the fungus cap that they became virtually invisible. Their mouths, equally hidden until opened, were directly beneath the front eyes and extended all the way back to beneath the side eyes. Triple rows of jagged teeth lined both jaws all the way around. There were no apparent ears.

"I didn't ask for a lecture," Quill said angrily. "I simply asked who you are and why you've bound us this way."

"I, personally, am Myco. We, as a group, are a Bluggia militia company, of which I am Captain, and we have only recently been called into active duty by King Krumpp. We, as a race, are Tripodians, one of the three dominant species in Bluggia, and are believed to have originated in the Chalkyn Desert of the Great Unknown Lands, to the east of Bluggia. As to who we are in the grand scheme of the infinite cosmos, that is hardly for us to say. And as for why we have bound you up like this — well, you can consider yourselves extremely fortunate that, so far, it is the only inconvenience you've experienced. Under normal circumstances, we would simply have devoured you when you sat upon us, since we are essentially carnivorous."

"Let's do it, Captain!" urged the Tripodian holding Kestra, his teeth clicking menacingly.

"Yes!" agreed the one holding Barnaby. "I'm starved!"

"Absolutely!" chimed in the one holding Kite. He was evidently going to say more, but Captain Myco blinked his large dark eyes rapidly several times in an angry way, silencing him.

"As it is," their leader went on, "we have no choice but to follow our instructions. We have taken you prisoner under direct orders from King Krumpp to bring any captured trespassers to Black Castle straightaway. He had a hunch you might be approaching this way and he very much wants you alive. We are even required to afford you protection as we do so. However," he added, his eyes glittering in the firelight, "he also bestowed upon me certain discretionary powers: If, in my estimation, you dare to make any further effort at resistance or disobey my orders in any way, I have the authority to order these troops to dine on you."

"Right!" said the Tripodian restraining Kestra. "And, in my opinion, they're resisting right now."

"Sure!" chimed in the one holding Kite, who was sitting perfectly still in his bonds. "Look how this one is fighting to get loose."

"I agree," agreed the one holding Quill. "Who could say otherwise if we reported that they resisted?"

"Of course you'd say that," put in the one holding Ergot, "when the one you've got is a nice meal. This little bit of nothing I've got would hardly be half a bite."

"Thank you, you're quite correct," murmured Ergot, for once not complaining about his size. "Besides, the probabilities are high that I wouldn't taste very good."

A whole chorus of voices erupted from the surrounding Tripodians then, agreeing that the prisoners should be eaten under the justification that they had resisted.

"Silence!" Captain Myco roared, silencing them. He was not all that opposed to eating them, since he was sure they'd be delicious, but he was also aware that there could well be a promotion in store for him for bringing in these prisoners unharmed. Fortunately for the captives, ambition took precedence over appetite, and he continued addressing his troops in a tone that would tolerate no argument: "We're taking them to Black Castle and that's that! Search that pouch." He used one of his fuzzy strands to indicate Kestra's large neck pouch lying on the ground nearby.

Three of the Tripodians came forward and dug eagerly through the pouch, tossing out packets of wafers and bags of *metta-metta*. These were all broken open and their contents distributed as equally as possible among the Tripodians, who began eating them with much crunching and slurping. Lara and Barnaby thought the eating habits of these fungus people were very impolite, since none of them took small bites or chewed with closed mouths, as the twins had been taught to do. In fact, the Tripodians' chewing was so noisy that Barnaby took a chance on not being overheard and spoke in an urgent whisper to his sister.

"Lara, for crying out loud, can't you cast *some* kind of a spell to get us out of this?"

"We do seem to be in a bad spot," Quill interjected in a whisper.

Lara nodded and directed her whispered response to the Dwarf. "I'm just glad we didn't bring the *Secret Volumes* with us."

Quill made a small sound of agreement at that, but Barnaby was clearly exasperated and muttered sourly, "Fat lot of good it's done us, your becoming a sorcerer."

"Better not talk, Barnaby," she whispered back. "It might give them the excuse they need to eat us."

Barnaby sighed and lapsed into silence while the Tripodians noisily finished eating.

Quill, however, groaned aloud as he saw that in these few moments their entire two-week food supply was gone. The sound caused one of the nearby Tripodians to stare at him, and Quill wisely became very silent.

Myco gave the empty food pouch a hard kick with his middle leg-stem, lofting it off the ledge and into the darkness beyond. After a moment they heard it hit far below. Then he kicked the burning sticks in the same way, causing them to loop away off the ledge and into the darkness below in little trails, like a fireworks display. Satisfied, he barked orders for strict silence to be observed by everyone and for the company to head for Black Castle. Without further ado, the march began, the captives still bound and riding in sitting positions — except for Ergot — on the rounded tops of the Tripodians.

They moved slowly at first, mainly because they were descending the steep slope on the northeast side of the high ledge. The ground, Lara saw, was strewn with loose rocks, making it treacherous going, even for the three-legged Tripodians. It was also apparent to Lara that the

Tripodians could see at least as well as she in this darkness, for they carefully walked around large rocks and
avoided falling into clefts or walking into the numerous
stunted trees or the occasional giant trees that towered
far above.

At one point, however, after they'd been descending
for a half-hour or more, one of the Tripodians near the
rear of the column stubbed a stem on a large rock and
inadvertently cried, "Ouch!"

Without warning a terrible screeching sounded directly above them and Lara couldn't help gasping as she
saw a pair of voracious Vulpines enter her field of vi-
sion, diving toward where the sound had originated.
There were hoarse cries from the Tripodians as they
quickly ducked behind rocks or trees to elude the great
birds, but not all were lucky enough to find protective
cover. First one, then another of the scurrying creatures
was snatched up in those awful jaws, screaming and
kicking as they were carried aloft and out of sight.

The whole episode had taken less than a minute, but
it took Captain Myco a lot longer than that to get his
frightened troops settled down and on the move again.

"Don't you have any kind of defense at all against the
Vulpines?" Lara whispered to Myco.

She felt him shudder beneath her. "Not one that does
us any good until it's too late," he growled softly. "Our
flesh is quite poisonous. Stupid though the Vulpines are,
they realize that and so they usually avoid us, but there

are always some around who are more stupid than the others. They're the ones who think they can get away with eating us. They die when they do, as those two bird-brains will, but that doesn't help those among us who proved the point to them." He abruptly caught himself. "Why am I talking to you? You were ordered to keep quiet. Not another word!"

Their downhill progress continued, and when they finally reached the bottom, they were on the bank of the stream they had named Kite River, which flowed from the north. Downstream from them it merged with the Kestra River, which flowed from the west. Much closer, one of the giant trees had been cut to fall across the river, from bank to bank. Its branches had been trimmed off, and the trunk made a sturdy narrow bridge some ten feet above the surface of the rushing waters. The column moved across carefully in single file and then reformed three abreast. Now that they were on the east side of the Kite River, they were on much more level ground. First they traveled through broad prairies of coarse low grass like black wire, which was difficult for the Tripodians to walk through. It was not long, however, before they came to a well-traveled roadway of hard-packed earth.

It was at this point that Captain Myco spoke loudly. "All right, troops, no more dawdling. Pick 'em up and put 'em down — we're getting out of Vulpine territory and heading for the Bay of Nightmares. Let's go!"

The name of the place was unpleasant enough to make the captives shiver. Their new fears about this were quickly pushed aside by the wonder of what was occurring as a result of Myco's command. The Tripodians had been moving with a sort of shuffling gait, but now, heading northward on the road, they lifted their stems higher and faster and their speed increased until the three stems of each were moving so fast they almost disappeared, like the spokes on a rapidly turning wheel.

The air began whistling past with their increased speed, and in a short while Lara was sure they were moving along at least as fast as Kite and Kestra had carried them through the air — maybe faster. As they continued traveling northward, the prisoners realized that they were able to dimly see what was around them. The reason, they soon discovered, was that a pale blue moon was rising on the northern horizon. Actually, it wasn't rising at all, any more than the Mesmerian sun was setting when they left it behind. It was just as stationary as the sun, but the farther north they traveled, the higher it seemed to move up into the velvet black of the sky. At the end of another two hours, the Melanistican moon was every bit as high in the sky as the Mesmerian sun was when they were in Verdancia, and the six captives could see a considerable distance. The objects below were visible in various shades, from a surprisingly bright silvery blue to a deep blackish-blue, giving the entire landscape a weird and decidedly ghostly aspect.

Myco lifted the ban of silence off his troops and, as if waiting for just that, the Tripodians broke into a song as they progressed — an odd, ululating melody that rose and fell with intermingled joy and sadness; the words muffled or overlapped in such a way that they were not understandable to the captives, yet they carried a haunting charm.

"Aren't you concerned that the sound will attract more of the Vulpines?" Lara asked Myco.

"Vulpines rarely venture this far north on their own," he replied. "They don't like moonlight any more than they like sunlight. The only Vulpines we'll see here are the mercenaries employed by King Krumpp, and we don't have to fear them, because they're —" He broke off and made a grumbling sound. "Why am I talking to you?" he asked himself. "More to the point, why are you talking to me? I lifted the silence ban from the troops, not from the prisoners. Be quiet!"

Lara did not respond, and for a long while the only sounds were the singing of the troops and the whirring of their stems on the road. Occasionally they passed through small towns and one fair-sized city without pause and then the road they were following turned in a great curve toward the east. In response to a whistling sound from Myco, the company of Tripodians began slowing. Soon the party could see the open expanse of a sizable body of water ahead of them. Their road swung north-ward again, following the shoreline, but Myco's company of Tripodians stopped. A smaller road, hardly more than a path, continued straight ahead, ending at a wharf at the water's edge.

"You six," Myco said, indicating the half-dozen Tripodians who had been traveling closest to the six carrying the captives, "stay with us. The rest of you," he raised his voice somewhat, "can continue up the road to Bluggburg. You're granted liberty there until summoned. That will probably not be until these prisoners are questioned by King Krumpp and then executed."

There were cheers from the majority of the troops at his announcement, along with an unhappy, barely audible grumbling from those who were still on duty and who watched enviously as their fellows scurried away up the road. There was also a considerable increase of fear in the minds of the captives as the significance of Myco's last remark sank in. They had thought they might be thrown in a dungeon, but had not even considered they might be executed.

In a few minutes more, the prisoners found themselves being carried across the wharf's heavy planking, heading directly toward where a small boat was moored. Across the expanse of water was the dark bulk of a large island on which were four mountains in a row. Atop the highest of these loomed a huge black structure with tall towers, its few windows glowing faintly yellow-green.

The party halted by the boat, and suddenly the fuzzy strands imprisoning the captives to the tops of the Tripodians were withdrawn. All six of them slid to the wharf, the swords of Barnaby and Quill clattering as they hit the wood. The prisoners lay or sat there groaning and rubbing their arms and legs to restore the circulation.

"All right, Mesmerians," Myco rasped, "unhook those weapons and leave them there. And get on your feet. The free ride is over."

The swords and dagger were laid aside cautiously, but Lara did not lay down the Wand. She was first to regain her feet, wincing as she stood up. She helped Barnaby rise and then scooped up Ergot in her free hand. The Shrood was trembling, though whether from fear or anger she couldn't tell. She handed Ergot to Barnaby, who placed him in his shirt pocket. By then, Quill, Kestra and Kite were also standing, stretching arms and legs and wings that had become cramped from such long confinement. Lara turned and faced Captain Myco, her brows drawn down.

"Since, from what you said, we are going to be executed anyway," she said, "then it really doesn't make any difference whether we speak or not. I want to know something."

"What?" Myco asked suspiciously.

"Is this the Bay of Nightmares?"

"Yes, and that's Grunda Island over there, where we're taking you."

"And that big building on the mountain?"

"That," replied Myco, chuckling deeply, "is Black Castle. And that's where you and your friends are going to have a nice little visit with King Krumpp."

"Then there's only one word I have to say to you and *your* friends, Captain Myco."

"And what is that?" he sneered.

She drew herself up, pointed the Wand at him and spoke a single word.

"*ELOCA!*"

13

The Black Castle

THERE WAS AN instant of shock reflected on Myco's face as Lara uttered the spell-word and the next moment he and his eleven men vanished.

"You did it, Lara!" Barnaby said. "You destroyed them!"

"Not likely," Ergot said, his head poking out of Barnaby's pocket, his long snout wrinkling as he sniffed the air. "Lara has chosen good sorcery over evil, and good sorcery does not lend itself to the destruction of anyone. Logic dictates that she has merely displaced them."

"That's true," Lara agreed. "Captain Myco and his men are at this moment back on Ergot's Ledge, and they're very confused. They won't be able to find their way for several days, so it will undoubtedly be some time before they are able to get back here."

"Well, I'm glad they're gone," Quill said. "My old bones ache."

"When did you realize your sorcery power had come back again, Lara?" Kite asked.

She shook her head. "It was never lost."

"But . . . but, Lara," Barnaby stammered, "you let us be held prisoner for such a long time! Why?"

"Think about it," piped up Ergot. "If she had used her powers any sooner, we would still have been in the dark — literally as well as figuratively — with no idea of where we were or where to go. By letting Captain Myco and his troops bring us here, and even protect us on the way, she saved us a lot of trouble, or maybe even disaster."

"Well, you could have let us know," Barnaby grumbled. "It wasn't very nice to let us be afraid for so long."

"I'm sorry, Barnaby," she apologized, "but it was necessary that the Tripodians believed we were really in their power. Otherwise they'd never have brought us here."

"I guess that was pretty smart of you to do as you did, Lara," said Kite, "but we have to admit we were a little worried."

"Yes," Kestra said. "For ourselves, of course, but even more for Mag Namodder. We thought we had failed. Come to think of it," she admitted, concern creeping back into her voice, "we haven't succeeded yet. What are we going to do now, Lara?"

A small smile touched the girl's lips and she was amused at how, by unspoken agreement, she had become leader of their party. She glanced at the Shrood. "Ergot, how do you evaluate the situation at this point?"

The Shrood closed his tiny eyes for a moment, then opened them and spoke in measured tones. "Mag Namodder is still alive and, most probably, so are King Daw, Queen Roo-Too and possibly even Rana Pipian. They are in the deepest dungeons of Black Castle, where they are closely guarded. All are in poor health, although Mag Namodder is the most seriously ill."

"There's no way you can know that, Ergot," Quill said skeptically.

"Here we go again," Ergot rumbled. "I suppose that means you have to know how I've come to that conclusion. Sure, sure, don't trust the little guy, no matter how many times he proves himself. It's always the way."

"I don't think he meant he didn't trust you," Barnaby said.

"How *do* you know, Ergot?" Quill persisted.

Ergot sighed. "It's all so elementary. All the information we have points to the fact that Mag Namodder, King Daw, Queen Roo-Too and Rana Pipian were imprisoned by Krumpp. All are great enemies of Krumpp and so that imprisonment had to be for one of two reasons — either to extract information from them or to keep them under control because he fears them. We can eliminate the first reason because either he would long ago have gotten the information from them that he wanted or he would have come to the conclusion that he would never get it from them. In either case he would thereupon have had them killed. Since Lara has assured us that he did not have them — or at least Mag Namodder — killed, then we must assume that the reason he kept them alive is either that he cannot or must not kill them. Since he has the *power* to kill them or have someone else kill them and has not exercised that power, then it becomes obvious that he *must* not kill them, because to do so would be detrimental to him or his powers. Since he has not set them free, this indicates that a danger exists for him if they are not under his control. Therefore, since he cannot murder them, or have them killed, and he cannot turn them loose, then he must keep them imprisoned until they die of natural causes — if you can call that natural. Since they are of such great concern to him, it stands to reason he would want them kept where they would have the least chance of escaping and where he can check on them often. Since he is an evil sorcerer and must get his power from some outside source, he knows the same is true with a good sorcerer like Mag Namodder and, being a sorcerer of considerable accomplishment, he undoubtedly knows that Mag Namodder's source of power is light. He would therefore wish to keep her the farthest away he could from any light source, which would mean in the deepest dungeon. Since it would be inconvenient to keep the prisoners in different locations, all of them are undoubtedly kept in the same area. Since they have been imprisoned there for hundreds of years, undoubtedly with poor or nonexistent care and only enough food for bare survival, then all would undoubtedly be ill, with Mag Namodder most seriously afflicted because she has been deprived of her power source. Since Krumpp would want to check on them often, and their continued captivity is important to him, they would be well guarded at all times in the deepest dungeon of the castle that is his headquarters. That, of course, is Black Castle. Thus, it seems to me we have to get into the castle over there as quickly and quietly as possible, head for the deepest, darkest dungeon and start searching. Does that answer your question, Quill?"

Quill sniffed. "Well, of course," he blustered, "it's all so *simple* if you're going to put it that way."

"We've got to get over there at once," Lara said. "Quill, Barnaby, you'd better get your weapons. Kite, Kestra, can you see well enough in just the moonlight to fly us across?"

"Yes," they answered in unison. "Whenever you're ready."

Within a minute Barnaby and Quill had restored their weapons to their belts and Lara had disengaged the Wand from her wrist and hung it about her neck so that it was hidden inside the front of her dress. They took their places as before on the Kewprums and, at a signal from Lara, the hawks took off.

"Ohhh, it feels good to be flying again!" Kestra sighed.

"I'll second thát," Kite said. "Where do you want to try to gain entry to the castle, Lara?"

She shook her head, realized he couldn't see that and said, "I don't know. I guess we'll just have to look it over and see."

That's exactly what they did. The Kewprums flew close together a dozen feet over the dark water of the Bay of Nightmares at first, staying low to help avoid detection. They quickly discovered the error of this when the water below them erupted in a tremendous splash and a huge creature, its body like a shark's and its great scaly head like a crocodile's, leaped upward at them. Its gaping jaws slammed closed in a great snap just below Kestra, so narrowly missing that she felt the whoosh of movement on the feathers of her underside.

"Climb! Climb!" she cried, and climb they did. By the time they reached the near shore of Grunda Island, they were about a thousand feet high, which put them on a level with the top of the tallest peak and at the base level of Black Castle, which perched there like some great, dark, brooding beast. That's where they began circling, making as little sound as possible now, so the only noise was a faint rush of wind over the wings of the Kewprums.

The castle was enormous, solidly built of massive carved blocks of stone so dark it looked like coal. A road spiraling up the mountain ended at the only apparent entry — a vast double door made of iron, strengthened by a latticework of reinforcing bands riveted in place. A smaller door was in one of the large doors, big enough only for an individual no larger than a Centaur to pass through. Two crepuscular Krins were there, evidently as guards, but both were hunkered down on their haunches, the wheezy buzz of their snoring distinctly audible.

"I wish we were home," Barnaby muttered in a frightened way.

"I do, too, Barnaby," Lara whispered back, no less scared than he. "This place gives me the creeps. I can't believe we're really trying to find a way to get *inside!*"

"We could just turn around and leave," Ergot piped up thinly. "Logic dictates that the odds of our getting in and out again safely — to say nothing of rescuing four people in the process — are no less than a thousand to one."

"Oh, Ergot!" Lara chided. "We wouldn't be able to live with ourselves if we did that!"

"I could," mumbled Barnaby, but so quietly that no one heard him.

"We can't just keep flying around out here," Kite said

softly. "Sooner or later someone's going to see us."

"Lara," Kestra said, "suppose we circle the whole cas-tle a few more times, going gradually upward. Maybe somewhere we'll find an entry. A large window, maybe."

"Good idea," Lara said, though her voice quaked.

Gradually upward they went and around and around Black Castle. There were a number of windows, but these turned out to be hardly more than slits, glowing from within with that same yellowish-green luminescence they had noticed earlier from the wharf. The big problem was that these window slits were so narrow that it was doubtful any of them except the Shrood could get through . . . and Ergot did not volunteer to try. At last, fully five hundred feet above the base of the castle, they reached the main part of the castle roof. A few towers and turrets soared as much as fifty feet higher, but they had no visible windows and there seemed no point in flying higher. If they were going to find an entry, the logical place seemed to be on the main roof. At a sug-gestion from Quill, the Kewprums glided to the most level surface and landed very quietly.

"We'd better spread out," Quill directed, his voice barely audible. "Tiptoe. Look for an entry. Whistle if you find one."

They moved apart, ghostly shadows on a ghostly roof and making no more noise than shadows. The roof was shingled and slightly pitched at different angles, but easy enough to move across if one walked carefully. They

quickly lost sight of one another among the different angles. Lara had hardly walked fifty steps when she came to a flat dormerlike structure facing away from her. She walked around it and found a sort of platform, level, circular and perhaps ten feet in diameter, an exact X dividing it. The dormer, facing out onto it, had a door faintly outlined with light showing through the cracks.

Excited, she puckered her lips and whistled softly once, twice, three times. In less than a minute the others had silently joined her and they all stood in a cluster on the circular platform before the door.

"This is strange," Kite whispered, indicating the platform. "It's like a landing place for someone . . . or some *thing.*"

"And the door," Barnaby said. "Who knows what's on the other side?"

"Ergot?" prompted Lara.

"Nothing," said Ergot, from Barnaby's shirt pocket.

"What do you mean, 'Nothing'?" Quill asked, frowning.

"I was asked what's on the other side. I answered: Nothing. The basic structure is no more than a facade, indicating that there is no available space for anything on the other side. The door is a false door. The glow of light showing through the crack serves no apparent purpose other than to act as a lure to attract someone to it."

"As it has attracted us?" Kestra asked.

The Shrood nodded. "Exactly. As it has attracted us."

"But *why?*" Barnaby asked.

"Could it be a trap?" Lara asked nervously.

"Not only could be," Ergot replied, "but logic dictates that this is precisely what it is."

Quill's shaggy brows went up and his eyes widened. "Then let's get away from —"

He didn't finish, because at that instant the circular platform they were standing on fell away below them in four sections along the lines of the X, plunging them into lightless empty space.

14

Krumpp

LARA SCREAMED, BARNABY and Quill yelled loudly and the mournful rumble of Ergot's voice could be heard from Barnaby's pocket, as they tumbled into the unknown. Kite and Kestra screeched and tried to use their wings, but the opening into which they had all plunged had quickly narrowed into a smooth tube too narrow for them to open their wings all the way. While the fall lasted only a few seconds, it seemed much longer to all of them.

Down and down they tumbled, the fall made even worse by the lack of visibility and their vivid imaginings of what would happen when they hit bottom, wherever that would be. Thoughts raced through Lara's mind as she sought to recall a spell that might help them, but she was still too inexperienced as a sorcerer and none of her elementary magic skills were of any value in this situation. She tried to withdraw the Wand from inside the front of her dress, but it became entangled and she could not. She remembered that when Warp fell from the cliff in Twilandia, he had screamed the spell-word *Ornitha*, which would have given him the power of flight. It hadn't worked for him because he had depleted all his available spell-power, but she tried it anyway.

"*Ornitha!* . . . *ORNITHA!*" she cried, but it was a Higher Level spell and she was unable to invoke it.

Abruptly they plunged into a vast room eerily lighted by walls glowing that muted yellow-green. Instantly they became enshrouded in a springy netting material that gave with their weight, slowing, slowing, slowing them until they stopped. Before they could collect themselves, the supports holding the material drew closed high over their heads and they were jumbled together in a mesh bag suspended only a feet feet above the floor of the great room.

"Owww!" cried Barnaby. "Somebody's elbow is in my ribs!"

"Ooof!" grunted Quill. "Get that knee out of my stomach!"

"Urgg!" gurgled Kite. "Whose arm is wrapped around my neck?"

"Oooh!" gasped Kestra. "I can hardly breathe!"

"Uhhh!" mumbled Lara. "Someone's leg is across my face!"

Only Ergot said nothing, not only because he hadn't been hurt, other than being bumped around a little, but because his rapid analysis of the situation suggested it would be wise to keep his presence in Barnaby's breast pocket hidden as long as possible.

A pervasive tittering and giggling was echoing throughout the room. It came from hundreds upon hundreds of furry black creatures seated on row after row of benches at long, low narrow tables on the hewn rock floor. A closer look showed them to be large, scruffy rats, each about the size of a small cat. Their amused sounds increased the more the captives struggled. Closer to the walls were standing a large number of other beings — Gnomes and Tripodians and Krins and Vulpines and several other species. They, too, were greatly amused and their chuckles and cackles and whoops added to the general din.

"Everybody — especially you stupid Blakkrats — quiet!" The command was given in a thin, reedy voice that carried the sharp ring of authority. As if a spigot had been turned, all the sounds of merriment ceased instantly.

"Well, well, well," said the same voice, "how nice of you to drop in!"

Again a roar of laughter swept the assemblage at the double meaning, then cut off sharply when the speaker made a chopping motion with his hand. Inside the mesh bag, the captives squirmed about until they were in positions where they could see the individual whose commands were so swiftly obeyed.

He was a tall man, clad in a belted floor-length robe. His shoulder-length hair and eyebrows were very black, as was his mustache and beard, cut in short, pointed Vandyke style. His small eyes were dark, piercing; his sharp nose overhanging a mouth from which protruded prominent, chisel-like, ochre-stained upper teeth, giving his entire face an unpleasant, pointed aspect. A peculiar aura surrounded him — a pale, electric-blue glow that made his outline nebulous while, at the same time, imparting a sense of tremendous power. On his right thumb he wore a ring set with a multifaceted, brilliant yellow gemstone and in his left hand he held a foot-long

cylindrical rod, yellow-orange in color and about twice the diameter of an ordinary pencil.

None of the captives had ever seen this person before, but they had no doubt they were finally face to face with the feared sorcerer, King Krumpp, ruler of Bluggia and conqueror of Mesmeria.

"Yes," he rasped, verifying their recognition of him, "I am Krumpp! How ridiculous for you to have had the *audacity* to think you could enter Black Castle by stealth!" He paused and took a small bite from the top of the rod in his left hand. "Did you really think," he continued, talking around the substance in his mouth, "that you could merely slip in here and rescue the witch, Mag Namodder, and her three puppet leaders from my deepest and most secure dungeon?" He took another bite from the rod.

Barnaby angrily thrust his arm through the netting and pointed a trembling finger at the King. "You are a *very* bad person! You have no right to hold Mag Namodder, to say nothing of King Daw and Queen Roo-Too and Rana Pipian. And you have *no* right to —"

Krumpp lifted his right hand and returned Barnaby's point. "*Sordo!*" he barked.

Barnaby's mouth clamped shut involuntarily and try as he might to open it, he could not. Nor was he the only one so affected. The mouths of Kite and Kestra and Quill were similarly locked shut. All the creatures in the room applauded loudly as the boy rolled his eyes in mute appeal toward Lara. The King let the applause continue until he finished taking another bite from the yellow rod. Then he changed his pointing finger to an open palm gesture toward the room, stopping the noise.

"I have neither time nor inclination to listen to *any* of you," he said sharply, "except for the girl, who has evidently become your leader by virtue of having a limited ability to perform magic. You," he said, pointing at Lara, "will be very wise to refrain from attempting any of your amateurish magic tricks here. I warn you, whatever spells you might try to invoke will be turned back on you a hundredfold. Do you understand?"

"Yes, sir," Lara replied, frightened.

"Good, good!" He took another bite of the yellow rod, which was now only half as long as when he began, and motioned with the index finger of his ringed hand toward a Gnome standing along the wall near some ropes attached to the netting holding the captives.

The Gnome bowed low and then tugged on two of the ropes in turn. At the first tug, the net containing Lara and the others lowered even more, until they were only a foot above the floor. The second tug caused the bottom of the mesh bag to open, dumping them out onto the floor. At once the material snapped back up against the high ceiling. Carefully, fearfully, the captives came to their feet and stood in a silent cluster facing the King. He made an imperative gesture and at once several of the guards darted in and relieved the captives of their weapons. Lara was suddenly glad she had been unable to withdraw the Wand during their fall.

"Now, then," Krumpp said brusquely, his piercing eyes locked on the girl, "you will answer my questions. You will answer them all, you will answer them fully and you will answer them truthfully. If you do not, you will die an especially horrible death — *all of you!* On the other hand, if you comply to my satisfaction, you will be allowed to live, even though it might be in a dungeon for the rest of your lives. First of all, who are you?"

"My name is Lara," she replied, her voice trembly. "This," she touched the shoulder of her twin, "is my brother, Barnaby. This," she indicated the old Dwarf, "is Quill, and the two Kewprums are Kestra and Kite."

"You are the ones who broke into Castle Thorkin?"

"We did not break in," Lara objected. "We simply walked in. That is, Barnaby and I did. These other three waited outside."

"You two just *walked* in, without being seen?" Krumpp sneered. "I warned you about lying to me!"

"I'm not lying! We were invisible and slipped in when some Centaurs opened the door."

"Invisible! Hmmm, very interesting. We'll get back to that little tidbit later. You and your brother are the ones who went up to the tower storage room?"

"Yes, sir."

"What did you take from there?"

"Nothing."

"You lie! I warned you about that!" The King pointed a long finger at Kestra and said, *"Ignes!"*

The hawk uttered a muffled moan as she became a solid cylinder of wax coated with her brushed-copper plumage, a thick twisted wick projecting from the top of her head. At the same moment the wick burst into flame and Kestra became a giant lighted candle.

The assemblage applauded and cheered wildly and joined Krumpp in the laughter that burst from him at the horrified expressions on the faces of Lara, Quill, Barnaby and, most of all, Kite. Once again, all sounds ceased as the King raised his hand.

"That is a sample," he told Lara coldly, taking another bite from the yellow rod, "of what will happen each time you lie. So long as the flame is burning, your Kewprum friend can be restored. Once it burns itself out, she will be gone forever. I promise to restore her if your answers satisfy me hereafter. The truth now! You and this boy *did* leave that storage room with two large books, did you not?"

"Yes, sir."

"Ah, that's better. You see, I know when you are lying and when you're not. The books were hidden up there in the tower?"

Lara hesitated, then nodded. "Yes, sir."

"What were the titles of these books?"

"They didn't have titles."

An angry glint came to Krumpp's eyes. "Just can't keep

Gradually upward they went and around and around Black Castle. . . . The big problem was that the window slits were so narrow that it was doubtful any of them except the Shrood could get through . . . and Ergot did not volunteer to try (page 140).

*"Look at your friends!" Krumpp rasped. . . . "Will you let them die?
I leave you here to contemplate such folly as you watch their lives slowly
burn away" (page 158).*

from testing me out, eh?" He pointed at Kite and Quill, invoking his spell twice, and, as Kestra had before them, both became oversized burning candles, the one that was Kite coated with feathers, the one that was Quill clad in the clothing Quill had been wearing.

"Uhhhhh!" Barnaby moaned behind closed lips. He was very pale and fearful, knowing he would be next if Krumpp even *thought* Lara had lied.

"Answer me!" Krumpp demanded. "Were those the *Secret Volumes of Warp?*"

"Yes," Lara said in a small voice.

"Have you or any of your friends here read them?"

"They . . . they . . . didn't. There was a warning on the first page. It frightened them."

"And what about you? Have you read the *Secret Volumes of Warp?*"

Lara thought of the third volume that they had not been able to take with them and she shook her head. "I . . . looked at some, but . . . no . . . no, I didn't actually read all of the *Secret Volumes.*"

Krumpp smiled faintly at that as he finished pushing the remainder of the rod he had been eating into his mouth. Automatically he reached inside his robe and brought forth another, just like the first, and took a bite from it. "Good, good!" he said.

She knew he wasn't talking about the material he was eating. A glance at the others showed that already the candle that was Kestra had burned down to the neck and those that were Quill and Kite had burned to their brows and there was a look of mute pleading in their eyes.

"Now," Krumpp went on, swallowing noisily and taking another bite, "we come to some very important questions. Answer very carefully, I warn you. Where are the two books you took from Castle Thorkin?"

"Hidden," Lara said promptly.

"Where?" His brows had pinched down.

"In Rubiglen."

"Don't toy with me, little girl. My patience is about gone. *Where* in Rubiglen?"

There was a moment of expectant silence broken only by the faint sputtering of the candles that were Kestra, Kite and Quill. Lara was trembling and her face had drained of color, but she stared into Krumpp's eyes and answered in a strong voice. "I won't tell you!"

"*IGNES!*" Krumpp shouted, pointing at Barnaby, who became a boy-sized burning candle clad in boy's clothing. The King swung his gaze back to Lara and spoke in a furious hiss: "*Tell me where in Rubiglen they are hidden!*"

"Go suck a lemon!" Lara retorted.

Krumpp had no idea what a lemon was, but her reply made him so angry that he chomped away half of the yellow rod in his hand before he was able to speak again. He signaled to a company of a dozen Gnomes standing along the nearest wall and they came to him at once, their expressions fearful.

"Pick them up," he ordered, indicating the burning candles. "We're going to the dungeons. Be careful! Hold them upright and don't let the flames go out. I want her to watch them burn down to their deaths. Maybe after one or two are gone she'll be more willing to talk."

The individual Gnomes were considerably smaller than the living candles, but they put their heads together and quickly devised a way of carrying them. They separated into four groups of three Gnomes for each candle. By stretching out their arms and clasping hands, each group was able to lift its candle straight up and, with much grunting and groaning, begin carrying it from the room. It was most difficult for them but, Lara noticed, none complained. Krumpp watched them approvingly as they threaded their way past the crowded tables. Then he strode toward Lara and grasped her wrist in a grip so hard she had to stifle a cry. Tears sprang into her eyes, but she bit her lower lip to keep from losing control. He jerked her after him, moving through the room with such rapid strides that she nearly had to run to keep up. Once she stumbled, but he didn't care; he simply dragged her along until she was able to get her feet under her again.

Krumpp passed the four laboring groups of Gnomes and then led the way out of the large hall into a corridor. They walked a long way until Krumpp stopped at the top of a flight of broad stone steps leading down into darkness.

"You two," he said, indicating the first two groups of

candle-bearing Gnomes as they reached him, "lead the way down. We'll follow. Then you two," he indicated the two remaining groups, "follow us."

Dutifully, the first and then the second groups started down, which was even harder for them than the level walking had been, yet there were still no complaints, though several of the Gnomes sent angry looks in Krumpp's direction when he wasn't looking their way. As the second group started down, Krumpp laughed in an ugly, humorless way.

"Take a good look around, Lara-girl," he told her. "This corridor will be the last place you ever see without bars and chains if you don't tell me what I want to know."

He laughed again and jerked her after him down the steps toward the dungeon.

15

The Dungeons

THEY MOVED DOWN flight after flight of stairs, the air becoming more stale and dank and repulsive the deeper they went. Lara was weeping openly, and the sounds of her shuddering sobs echoed from the black stone walls.

"Stop that sniveling," Krumpp snarled, "or I'll silence you permanently!"

Lara continued weeping . . . soundlessly. She was deeply afraid and berated herself for getting the others into this. They had looked to her for strength and protection because she had studied the *Secret Volumes of Warp*. And this was how she helped them? Whatever confidence she had experienced early in their expedition was gone; she was terrified of the awesome powers of Krumpp, which were obviously so much stronger than her own. Her weeping now was not so much that she feared for her own life — though, of course, she did — but because she knew she had failed those who had trusted in her, and equally because the mission to rescue Mag Namodder had flopped.

Now her brother and their friends had been turned into candles, and minute by minute their lives were burning away. She probed her memory of what she had read in the books, searching for some spell she could invoke that would put out the flames consuming the others, a spell that could return them to their usual selves, but there was none she could recall. Her despondency increased.

Their way down the stairs was lighted at intervals by burning pools of oil in saucerlike containers carved into the walls, but such open lamps were few and had it not been for the illumination shed by the four candles, it would have been much darker and more dangerous going. Three times as they continued downward they passed corridors branching away through arched openings. Gnomes and Trolls and a few Centaurs and scores of Blakkrats were on guard, standing their posts in a re-signed way or patrolling back and forth before long rows of iron doors with small barred portholes. The guards became very alert as the procession passed, but Krumpp only nodded at the Gnomes and Centaurs and pointedly ignored the Trolls and Blakkrats. No one spoke. Lara deduced that the corridors were different levels of dungeons and, in the midst of her own concern and fear, she wondered what poor souls were locked up in these rooms and what crimes, if any, they had committed. At last they reached the bottom, by which time Lara had managed to stop crying, and were immediately approached by the five guards there — one elderly bearded Centaur, three Warted Gnomes and a Troll. The Centaur, who carried a metal hoop upon which were a dozen or more keys, was in charge. The three Gnomes had warts all over their hands and faces — a characteristic of their subspecies. Each of the three carried a short whip tipped with a spiked ball. The Troll, who was the first of his kind Lara had seen at close range, was incredibly ugly. His brow was heavy, hairy, overhanging protuberant slime-green eyes. The fat shapeless nose hung to his chin and helped to hide a broad, slobbering mouth. He had a growth of scraggly, filthy black hair in wild disarray all over his body except for his face, the palms of his knobby hands and the soles of his widely splayed feet. Adding to his repulsiveness was a nauseating stench that nearly made Lara sick.

"Number Five," Krumpp ordered curtly, taking a bite from a fresh yellow rod.

The Centaur bobbed his head and led them — the Gnomes and Troll falling in behind — down the dismal corridor, passing numerous numbered doors as they walked. Before reaching the end, they stopped in front of a scabrous rusted door with the number 5 above its barred porthole. The Centaur opened it with one of his keys and stood aside with his fellow guards as the twelve huffing and perspiring Gnomes carried the four burning candles into the room and relievedly set them down. It was a windowless room, not much bigger than a large closet, with no furniture and only a scattering of straw on the cold stone floor as bedding.

As soon as the dozen Gnomes scurried back out into the corridor to wait, Krumpp jerked Lara past him, thrusting her into the room so violently that she sprawled on the bumpy rock floor. She sat up, trying hard not to start crying again as she rubbed a painfully scraped knee.

"Look at your friends!" Krumpp rasped. The electric-blue aura that surrounded him pulsed with his anger. "Will you let them die? I leave you here to contemplate such folly as you watch their lives slowly burn away. Do not think you can put out the flames when I leave. Only *I* can do that."

He paused, looking at her intently from the open doorway, absently taking little nibbling bites from the yellow rod. He swallowed noisily and when he spoke again, his voice had softened a little. "Be reasonable, girl. None of this *has* to happen. I don't want to see them die, any more than you do. All you have to do is tell me where those books are hidden. That's not much to ask. Isn't that worth the lives of your friends?"

She looked up at him defiantly. "I don't believe you and I will *never* tell you that."

"Little fool!" he snarled. "We'll see about that. I'll be back in one hour, just before this one burns out." He pointed at Kestra, then swung his gaze back to Lara. "You'll never tell me, eh? I wouldn't count on that!" He stared at her menacingly and his next words were cold, implacable: "Think about spending the remainder of your days here knowing you could have saved them, but didn't."

The door clanged loudly as he slammed it shut. As it was being locked, Lara came to her feet. She crouched below the door's porthole and for a short while heard the muffled tones of Krumpp's voice as he spoke to the guards. Then came the sound of receding footfalls, followed by silence. But it wasn't really silence. Gradually terrible sounds touched her ears and sent new fear coursing through her. These were muted groans and cries of pain and the soft wailings of a multitude of other prisoners in distant cells. The little girl wondered if that was what the future held for them now — a lifetime of desolation, locked away in a tiny dungeon cell in the bowels of an enemy stronghold. Assuming, of course, that her friends were able to survive this ordeal of being burned away as candles. The terrible enormity of their predicament flooded her.

Lara leaned against the door, crying softly. Through

her tears she could see the candle that was Kestra had already burned down to nearly the midpoint. Those that were Kite and Quill had burned to the shoulders. More than half of Barnaby's head was gone.

"Well, this is a fine pickle we're in!"

The sudden voice made her gasp and then she saw Ergot's head poking out of the shirt pocket on the candle that was her brother.

"Oh, Ergot!" she wailed, coming to him at once and taking him into her hands. "What are we going to do? I mustn't tell him where the books are, but he's going to let Barnaby and the others die if I don't. And I can't stop him; his power is so strong it . . . it . . . *envelops* me when he's close. I'm so scared!"

"There, there," he said in a soothing rumble. Neither thought it strange that this tiny Shrood perched on Lara's thumb should be attempting to comfort her; it seemed quite the natural thing to do and it was working, too, because her sobbing diminished and soon she was able to give him a weak smile.

"Now, listen," he went on. "I heard everything that was said and saw most of what went on through Barnaby's buttonhole, so let's analyze this a bit." He stood up, clasped his hands behind him and walked in a meditative circle on her hand. Once he paused and murmured, "Tsk tsk," and another time he paused and said, "Hmmmmmm," and at length he jolted to a stop and looked at her directly.

"You said something earlier that may have considerable significance," he told her.

"I did?"

"Yes. You said King Krumpp's power is so strong it envelops you when he's close. Lara, he's *not* close now. I know he told you only *he* could put out the flames, but why not try anyway? What could it hurt?"

She nodded, brightening, and, placing Ergot on her shoulder, turned to face the candles. She stretched out both arms in a gesture that embraced the candles and then she spoke in an authoritative manner.

"*Kwinka!*"

The flames of the four candles had been remarkably steady since coming to life, but now they wavered, flickered, swayed — as if a gust of breeze had touched them — and squeezed down to half their previous height. But they remained lighted.

"Again!" Ergot told her, yanking on her hair in his enthusiasm. "Give it some real pizazz!"

"*KWINKA!*" Lara cried, putting all she had into the spell.

Again the flames flickered and swayed and this time they diminished to only a quarter their original size, but still they burned. Lara's face fell and she hiccuped, a sure sign she was on the verge of tears.

"Now listen here!" Ergot said, putting a bit of an edge to his voice. "Don't you go getting discouraged, Lara. You've got some neat powers, you know that! Not only what you picked up from the *Secret Volumes,* but you've got the Wand, too."

The Wand!

In the excitement of falling down the tube and being caught in the netting, of being interrogated by Krumpp and thrown into a dungeon, Lara had all but forgotten about the Wand hanging around her neck inside her dress. Now she eagerly felt for it, found it was still there and brought it out. She took it from around her neck and gripped it firmly in her left hand, thrilling to the sense of power that surged up her arm and flooded her. Without another word to Ergot, she raised the ball end of the Wand toward their companions and repeated the command without raising her voice.

"*Kwinka.*"

The clear ball of crystal swirled inside as if with roiling clouds of multicolored smoke and simultaneously the four candles snuffed out. The dungeon became much dimmer at once, though not entirely dark, since the swirling clouds within the ball continued glowing. The portion of the wicks that had burned away were reformed, as if never touched by flame, and the wax that had been burned away rebuilt itself completely in a matter of seconds. That was not the end of it: all semblance of the four having been candles vanished and they were once again themselves, none the worse for the experience.

"Oh, Barnaby! . . . Kestra! . . . Quill! . . . Kite!
. . . Oh, how wonderful to have you back." Lara was crying again, but no one minded at all, since these were tears of joy.

For a few minutes after that, everyone was talking at once and there was a lot of hugging and kissing and rubbing and back-patting and happiness. There was no need for her to explain what had happened, since all four had remained fully aware of what was going on. The Wand, having finished its task, had gradually lost its glow and Lara replaced it around her neck so that it hung out of sight inside her dress. The only light in the cell now was the faint illumination coming through the porthole from one of the oil lamps in the corridor wall. They hardly noticed. They were so overjoyed at Lara's success with the Wand that it was several minutes before they realized that not only were they still in a predicament, Krumpp would be returning before long. With that so-bering thought, their joy diminished.

"I'm . . . I'm worried," Lara admitted, "that, even with the Wand, we won't be able to overcome Krumpp's powers. I know the Wand is very powerful . . . in the right hands. But I'm still a very unskilled sorcerer and don't know how to use it to its full potential. And . . . and . . ." She broke off, sniffling.

"Lara," Quill said worriedly, "what is it? What's wrong? Are you keeping something from us?"

She nodded as she wiped her eyes. "The Wand is a powerful tool when used properly," she said, "but if used improperly or by someone who does not understand its potential, it can cause great harm, not only to the user, but to anyone else close by. It's so powerful and I'm so afraid of hurting us all by using it without really knowing what I'm doing."

"I sure wish we still had *our* weapons," Barnaby said gloomily. "Without them we have no way of even threatening Krumpp when he shows up again."

"We still have our talons," Kestra said, "Kite and I. Maybe we could attack him before he is able to defend himself. Maybe." She fell silent, realizing there was very little chance of this.

"Perhaps," Ergot spoke up, "it might be wise to stop worrying about Krumpp for the moment and give some thought to the whereabouts of Mag Namodder and the others."

"You're right," Quill said. "Chances are she and Daw and Roo-Too are —"

"Don't forget Rana Pipian," Kite interjected.

"Yes, of course," Quill amended, "Rana Pipian, too, if he's still alive. Chances are that they're all down here somewhere."

"That's probably true," Lara said, worry still heavy in her voice, "but there must be a hundred dungeon rooms on each level. Even if we get out of this one, how could we find the right one before Krumpp came back?"

"Elementary," said Ergot, still perched on Lara's shoulder. "And don't worry too much about whether Rana Pipian is still alive. The odds have improved considerably that he is."

"How could you ever come to that conclusion?" Kestra questioned.

"And how can it be elementary to find the right cell among all that are down here?" Barnaby asked.

Ergot sighed. "Here we go again," he grumbled. "No one ever takes the word of the little guy. Simple deduction explains it. Consider: There are four of them and we know that Krumpp imprisoned them in his deepest dungeon. Since we came all the way down to the bottom, then this is undoubtedly the deepest dungeon. Furthermore, since we have been placed in the cell marked number five, it is most likely that Mag Namodder, Daw, and Roo-Too are in cells numbered one, two and three. And since we were not put in cell four, the conclusion must be that it, too, is occupied; if so, then the odds are good that its occupant is Rana Pipian. Finally, don't you remember that before Krumpp turned you into candles, he asked how you had the audacity to think you could sneak into Black Castle and rescue Mag Namodder and her *three* puppet leaders? One . . . two . . . three — Daw, Roo-Too and Rana Pipian."

"Then they're only *feet* away from us!" Lara exclaimed, clapping her hands together under her chin.

"And that's exactly where they're going to stay!" said a loud voice.

They gasped and looked up to see the bearded Centaur guard staring at them through the door's porthole.

16

A Reunion . . . Sort of

"Y OU'RE IN A heap of trouble!" the Centaur told them in an ugly manner, his bearded face framed in the barred porthole in the iron door. Standing in a row on his broad back, craning to get a look into the cell, were the three Warted Gnomes.

"You tell 'em!" said the first.

"Right!" echoed the second.

"Big trouble!" agreed the voice of the third.

"What's happening?" asked the Troll peevishly, out of sight somewhere below them. "What'd they do? . . . What'd they do?"

"Reversed the candle spell somehow," the Centaur replied. "We've got to tell King Krumpp about this!" His face jerked away from the window and they heard the clatter of his hooves. "Lara," Ergot said quickly, "do something. Stop them . . . *now!*"

Lara wasted no time. "*Dehisce!*" she commanded.

The heavy iron door burst open, knocking over the Troll and sending him rolling backward until he jarred to a dazed stop with his back against the opposite wall of the corridor. With Ergot on her shoulder, Lara, followed by the others, rushed out and saw the Centaur and his three Warted Gnome riders far down the corridor, just approaching the stairs.

Though she had never cast the Spell of *Ossyfia,* Lara remembered it very well, since it was the very first spell she and Barnaby had ever experienced in Mesmeria, and she did not hesitate to invoke it now, pointing a steady finger at the retreating guards.

"*Ossyfia!*"

A brilliant ball of green light appeared on her fingertip and then sped toward the retreating guards, enveloped them in a green glow and paralyzed them from the neck down. "Terrific Lara!" Barnaby chortled. "Oh, that's just great."

But it was not all that wonderful, because even though the guards had become paralyzed, their voices remained unaffected and at once they began to yell. Without having dropped her pointing finger, Lara swiftly invoked another spell, learned less than an hour ago from Krumpp.

"*Sordo!*"

The mouths of the guards continued moving, but no more sound emerged from them. Lara turned her head and looked at Ergot only inches away on her shoulder. There was a thread of worry in her voice as she spoke to him. "Do you think they heard them upstairs?"

Ergot frowned as he analyzed the situation. Then he brightened. "Possibly, but I doubt it. Had they heard, almost certainly someone would have come by now. As for how long it will be before Krumpp returns, I have no good estimate. If he truly planned to return before Kestra burned out completely, he'll be back within another fifteen or twenty minutes."

"Then we'd better get busy trying to find Mag Namodder and the others," Quill said nervously. "I have to admit, I'd like to get our task finished and get out of this place as soon as possible."

"That's reasonable," Ergot commented.

"And maybe Lara ought to put the Troll under the spell, too," said Kite.

"That's reasonable too," Ergot agreed. He looked at Lara and she paralyzed the Troll with a murmured word.

"And," Barnaby put in, "we'd better get the ring of keys from that Centaur to unlock the cells."

"That's *not* reasonable," Ergot added, "considering that both Lara and Quill have the power to open doors on command. Lara?"

The girl nodded and led the way toward the deepest, darkest end of the corridor beyond the cell they had occupied. The door to that final cell was much heavier than the others had been and, instead of having an oversized lock as the others had, it was permanently sealed, not only with a latticework of iron bars but also with two massive square-cut timbers. There was no barred port-hole as in the other doors, and the only opening was a narrow slot at the bottom through which food and water could be passed. Motioning the others to stand back out of the way, Lara stretched both arms toward the door, summoning up her most commanding tone.

"DEHISCE!"

The grating rattled and the sealed door trembled and groaned, but remained in place. Lara looked stricken.

"I can't give it any more than that," she cried. "It's more than merely sealed. I think Krumpp has placed a spell of his own on it to prevent its being opened."

Ergot shook his head. "I hate to keep pointing out the obvious, Lara, but you *do* have the Wand. Surely it can dispose of any spell invoked here by Krumpp."

Lara nodded, looking somewhat abashed. "It's some-times hard for me to remember," she said, "that not only am I a sorcerer, but that my limited powers can, with care, be greatly enhanced by judicious use of the Wand."

She pointed the Wand at the door, noting as she did so something of which the others were not yet aware. The shaft of the Wand had grown warm in her grip and a tingling sensation, like a small electric shock, was running up her arm.

"*Dehisce*," she commanded, speaking in hardly more than a conversational tone. Instantly the phenomenal power of the Wand became evident again as a thunderous roaring filled the corridor and the thick door strained against its reinforcing bars and timbers. Jagged cracks appeared in the portal and the iron bars sagged as if having suddenly been brought to the melting point. The two square-cut timbers burst at their centers in a shower of splinters, as if struck by lightning, and the door broke apart, clanging and banging as the pieces flew into the corridor, struck the opposite wall and fell to the floor. The giant padlocks on Cells 2, 3, and 4 shattered as if made of glass and the doors blew outward, thrown off their hinges. Not only that, all the other cell doors between them and the steps — over ninety of them — came open with varying degrees of force, dependent upon how far away they were from Lara. The effect was an explosive, reverberating din.

"Now *that*," Ergot said mildly, "was probably heard on the next level up. We may now expect some visitors in the immediate future."

"I'll just have to learn to temper my commands when using the Wand," Lara said apologetically. "I always seem to do it either too hard or too soft. Maybe on this next one I can do it properly."

She murmured a multiple-word command and, as if a switch had been thrown, all the walls of the corridor and cells began glowing with pale yellow light. Up the full length of the corridor, individual prisoners — hesitant, fearful, dazed, wondering — were emerging from their cells.

Ergot, still on Lara's shoulder, nodded. "You there!" he called, his heavy voice rumbling with authority through the corridor. "You're free now, but prepare to defend both us and yourselves if you want to get out of here!"

The inmates began picking up chunks of wood or pieces of iron from the shattered doors to use as weapons. Those closest to the paralyzed guards relieved the four of their weapons. Then they began grouping together — a ragtag army ready to fight any odds to preserve their precious newly gained freedom.

"Good," the Shrood said, "they'll help keep the opposition occupied for a while. We'd better get busy."

Everyone seemed to know what to do without being told; Kite and Kestra immediately headed for Cell 4, Quill went to Cell 3, and Barnaby approached Cell 2. Lara, with Ergot, picked her way carefully over the debris and entered Cell 1. The interior was about the same as theirs had been and she stopped short at sight of a figure lying outstretched on the straw in a far corner.

It appeared to be the mummified remains of an incredibly old woman, but she bore no resemblance whatever to the person Lara had known as Mag Namodder. Her skin was like fragile parchment and just as yellowish-brown. Her nose was warty and veined and, because it nearly touched her bony chin, seemed overlong. Actually it wasn't, but the loss of all her teeth had caused the mouth to collapse inward. Her eyes were half-open, unseeing. What hair remained on her head was an ugly yellow-gray and so sparse that the ears seemed enormous. Only fragments of an ancient cowled robe covered her, and the exposed limbs were so thin that the hands and feet, though skeletal, appeared much too big. Long-fingered, knobby hands were folded across her breast. Her whole body was shrunken, tiny; so small that Lara shook her head.

"This . . . this can't have been Mag Namodder. She was a tall woman and her features were different. Even in death she couldn't've withered to this size . . . or look like this."

"Thank goodness for that," Ergot breathed. "Maybe that means we'll still find her."

"But I wonder who this was," the girl said softly, "and how long ago she died?"

There was the sound of footsteps at the doorway and then an unfamiliar voice cried, "Lara! It's really you!"

Lara spun around. Barnaby was there, but it was not he who had spoken; it was the man standing beside him — a middle-aged man, gaunt, but of stately bearing. For an instant she did not know him, and then recognition came in a flood.

"Daw! Oh, Daw!" She flung herself at her cousin and

he scooped her up and hugged her close, unable to speak, his eyes overflowing.

"And Roo-Too, also," said Quill, who had just come to the door with a badly malnourished but still attractive middle-aged woman with long red hair and pale blue skin.

"Roo-Too!" Daw choked out her name. He gently set Lara down and emotionally embraced the wife he had neither seen nor spoken to for centuries, though he had been within a few feet of her all that while.

In the next moment Kestra and Kite entered the doorway, helping to support between them an emaciated individual with bulbous eyes, his broad mouth set in a grin. It was a Freep, and a very familiar one at that. Despite his apparent weakness, Rana Pipian, the warrior frog, straightened and bowed respectfully to the twins and Daw.

"Your Majesties," he murmured in a choked voice, "I had thought never again to see you. I am overwhelmed."

"Oh, Rana Pipian, Roo-Too, Daw!" Lara sobbed. Barnaby was weeping, also, and the twins were trying to hug everyone at once. Lara's voice kept breaking. "It's so . . . so . . . *grand* seeing all of you again! It's so . . . so . . . Oh, there just aren't words for it!"

A growing commotion at a distance impinged on their reunion and Ergot cleared his throat gruffly. "I hate to always be the one to throw cold water on things," he said, "but a considerable fight is now occurring at the base of the stairs. Assuming that half the liberated prisoners of this dungeon level are neither too weak nor too disabled to fight, and are presently so engaged, and that they are using makeshift weaponry against swords and spears, even though against a smaller number of descending guards, the likelihood is pronounced that within approximately the tenth part of an hour these erstwhile inmates will be killed or at least driven back to this end of the corridor. That is, of course, assuming reinforcements for the guards do not arrive; and assuming further that Krumpp himself does not show up, in which latter eventualities the time frame of such a contingency will be markedly foreshortened."

"Who is *that?*" asked Rana Pipian, staring at the Shrood.

"What did he *say?*" asked Roo-Too.

"This is Ergot and he is a Shrood. He said," Lara explained, "that the prisoners we've freed cannot hold off the guards for more than another six minutes."

"We've *got* to find Mag Namodder!" Quill said urgently.

Daw was the one who replied to that, his voice now so low that they could barely hear him above the growing din. He pointed to the tiny, wizened figure lying on the straw in the corner.

"You *have* found her," he said sadly. "*That* was Mag Namodder."

17

Power of the Wand

THE SHOCK THAT Daw's words produced in the little group was intense. Lara and Barnaby turned pale and speechless. Silent tears dribbled from Quill's eyes and clung to his beard in tiny droplets. Kestra and Kite moved close together and leaned against one another, both of them trembling. A deep, inarticulate groan rumbled from Ergot. Daw, Roo-Too and Rana Pipian wore morose expressions and, like Quill, both Daw and Roo-Too were weeping. The commotion at the far end of the corridor seemed suddenly louder to the group in Cell 1. It was Barnaby, his voice unsteady with emotion, who finally spoke.

"How . . . long ago did she die?"

Daw shook his head. "I don't know. We always communicated by tapping on the walls, using a code we devised. It was often the only thing that kept us going — being able to communicate in that limited way. Then Mag Namodder's responses began falling off. She took longer to reply and her answers were shorter and I knew her strength was failing at last." He shook his head and wiped his eyes briefly with the back of his hand. "The last message was about a week ago. Just one word: 'Goodbye.' I tapped it out to Roo-Too, who relayed it to Rana Pipian."

Lara moved to the pathetic form in the corner and knelt. She straightened the straw upon which the body lay and smoothed the ragged remains of the robe. She brushed her hand gently across Mag Namodder's brow

and down the lined, leathery cheek. With her finger-
tips, she gently closed the sunken eyes. A spasm of
trembling wracked her and she buried her face in her
hands and wept silently.

"Lara . . . look!" It was the husky voice of the Shrood
on her shoulder.

The girl raised her head and looked at Ergot and then
to where he was pointing — at Mag Namodder. The eyes
that the girl had just closed with her fingers were slowly
opening again and at the outer edge of one eye a single
tear formed, then spilled over the lid.

"She's alive!" Lara breathed and then, with growing
excitement, *"She's alive!"*

They all rushed to gather around. Except for the half-
opened eyes and the one tear, there had been no change
and the old woman still looked dead. Then, as they
watched in disbelief, the wrinkled lips parted and the
mouth opened a little.

"Laaaaar . . . aaaaaa . . ."

It was scarcely audible; more the faint hissing of an
escaping breath, but there was no doubt of it: Mag Namodder had spoken. A surge of excitement filled them
all, but no one spoke, afraid any sound they made might
obliterate any faint whisper from her. The old lips did
not move, but the voice touched them again, like the
wisp of a memory.

"Laaaaar . . . aaaaa . . . It . . . is . . . you?"

"Yes, Mag Namodder, it is." The girl carefully lifted

one of the bony old hands and grasped it gently in her own. "We came to get you — to take you home. We thought we were . . . too late." Her voice broke.

"Too . . . late . . . Get . . . away . . . Get . . . away . . ."

"No, not without you!" Lara could hardly speak and her shoulders heaved with ill-contained sobs. All the others were crying silently.

"Get . . . away . . ." the whispery voice repeated. "Get . . . away . . . Go . . . now . . . He . . . will . . . destroy . . . you."

Lara patted the withered hand ever so gently and when she finally spoke again, she was more in control of herself. "No. We can't just go away. We have to fight him . . . his evil. We have a chance now, Mag Namodder. We . . . maybe we can stop him now. I've learned some of the skills — some of the spells."

The old eyes opened a fraction wider. Her shallow breath wheezed faintly through the unmoving lips as she tried to form words. "How . . . learned?"

"The books — the *Secret Volumes of Warp* — we found them! I've been learning. Mag Namodder, I crossed over. I am a First Level sorcerer now!"

The eye's opened even more and there was the faintest of quiver at the old woman's lower lip. "For . . . good." It was a statement, not a question, but Lara confirmed it.

"For good, yes! Never for evil. There's so much more

to learn! Maybe I have enough to stop Krumpp. Probably not, but we can't give up, *ever.*"

The fragile lips quivered more and turned up in the vaguest suggestion of a smile. "May . . . be . . . ," she wheezed, ". . . May . . . be . . . But . . . only . . . with . . ." She fell silent then and everyone in the room became conscious of the sound of the fight in the corridor growing louder as it came closer, the weak and poorly equipped defenders being driven back toward this far end of the dungeon.

Mag Namodder remained silent for so long that Lara was about to speak, but as she opened her mouth, the whispery voice came again. "One . . . day . . . Laaaar . . . aaa . . . Search . . . find . . ."

"What, Mag Namodder? Search for what? Find what?"

"Find . . . Wand . . ."

"We *found* a wand, Mag Namodder! It was with the books. I have it here!" Suddenly excited, she carefully disengaged her hands and drew the Wand from the front of her dress, took it off from around her neck and held it before the old woman's eyes. The warmth of it had increased and now the bulbous end had begun to glow. Lara continued speaking eagerly. "Can you see? Can you see it? Is this what you mean?"

For the first time a certain animation was manifested by the form on the straw; the faintest of voluntary movement of the shoulders, an unsuccessful effort to raise the head, the successful slight movement of one hand.

Slowly, the eyes opened more, nearly all the way, losing some of their vacuity, focusing to some extent on the Wand. All this accompanied by a long, drawn-out sigh. "You . . . always were . . . able to . . . surprise . . . me, . . . Laar . . . ra." A sound remotely like a relieved chuckle faltered past the withered lips and dwindled to only a memory. After a moment she continued: "Put . . . into my . . . hands . . . child."

As the others watched, fascinated, Lara, with evident relief at being able to turn the powerful tool over to someone skilled enough to handle it properly, cautiously wrapped the gnarled fingers around the shaft and arranged both hands so they were holding the Wand in a perpendicular position, the smooth crystal knob up. At once there came a change in the old woman — a suffusion of color to her skin and a lessening of the mummified appearance. There was a change in the Wand, too, an increased glow. Mag Namodder began to speak, not to Lara, but in a whispered mystical incantation that steadily increased in strength and rhythm. Her face became more animated and the lips moved with more facility, forming words with less hesitation and greater clarity, though they were words none of the group had ever before heard.

The knob of the Wand changed from a clear bluish glow to slowly swirling, cloudy blue-white, reminding Lara of the layer of brilliant clouds that had once lined the miles-high ceiling of Underland and brought vigorous life and health to Twilandia. The swirling chromatic clouds changed successively to violet and then lavender and then blushed rose. The more the color within the ball changed, the brighter it became, evolving from rose to brilliant crimson and quickly blending into a fiery red-orange. The room itself became a rainbow of moving colors, constantly merging, shifting, brightening, sending the shadows of the transfixed onlookers into a phantasmagoric dance across the walls. The red-orange became a vivid pure orange, then blossomed into an all but blinding yellow that became, finally, an intense, incandescent yellowish-green.

The color of the Mesmerian sun.

The light spilled into the corridor, bathing it with a brilliance such as it had never known. The sound of conflict tapered off and there were cries of fear and pain as this brilliant glow flooded large dark eyes accustomed to only the dimmest of light.

"If not notified previously of what's happening down here," Ergot murmured, more to himself than to the others, "which I doubt, Krumpp will know soon enough now. I give us two more minutes — tops."

"That should be enough."

The words, no longer weak and faltering, came from the figure lying on the bed of straw still holding the the Wand. The body of Mag Namodder was undergoing a transformation; withered flesh firming, smoothing, taking on a healthier glow; the shrunken frame straightening, filling out. Even the ragged cowled robe was rejuvenating, the rents sealing themselves into smooth textures, the fir needles of which it was originally woven becoming once again full and soft and delicate pale green. Nor were changes to Mag Namodder the only changes occurring. The awful gauntness of Roo-Too and Daw and Rana Pipian was fading, being replaced by the robust health the twins had always known them to have; the pallor caused by long confinement replaced by good color, their eyes bright and clear, their clothing gradually becoming fresh and clean and crisp.

The twins, the Kewprums, Quill and Ergot also felt some changes in themselves — a sense of well-being and sharp-mindedness; a sense of competency and self-confidence infusing them all.

Well before the two minutes were up the glow of the Wand faded and the knob at its end became again only a solid globe of clear crystal. Mag Namodder had become the beautiful, magnetically alive mature personality Lara and Barnaby had always known her to be. She sat upright and then came to her feet smoothly and gracefully, without assistance, her radiant smile embracing them.

Rana Pipian was first to speak. He was now clad in a short garment of expertly woven chain mail, so fine as to give the appearance of cloth, but so strong it could

repel the thrust of dagger or slash of sword with ease. He bowed low, his long muscular legs straight, his broad webbed feet slightly apart.

"Welcome back, Your Majesty. It has been a long and difficult time."

She went to him at once, embraced and kissed him, then did the same with all the others, even Ergot — which wasn't easy at all. The Shrood shuffled in an embarrassed way and then leaped to Barnaby's shoulder and ducked into his pocket.

"I had continued," she said, "to harbor hope for *so* long — for hundreds of years. But I also knew the odds were against anyone's being able to help. A sorcerer must be exposed to the source of his power or it ultimately fails, as did mine. As the years and decades and centuries passed, all my powers diminished until the only hope remaining was that somehow, in some way, I would be delivered from this darkness and brought again into the Mesmerian sun. I never conceived it possible that the power could be restored to me here. Now it has been, thanks to you. She held up the Wand. "With this — which I had never thought to see again after Warp stole it and hid it away before he was killed — a great many things are possible. It is not invincible," she hastened to add, "but it does help us immeasurably.

"One day, Lara," she went on, stooping and putting her arm around the girl, "you must tell me how you found it — how you even knew where to look."

"It was Barnaby who knew," Lara said quickly. She smiled at her brother and at the look of appreciation he gave her and went on: "At least he remembered where Daw had once told him the *Secret Volumes of Warp* were hidden and so we went there and found them. And that's where the Wand was, too."

Mag Namodder extended the Wand toward Lara. "It's yours, child," she said. "No one has greater claim now than you."

"Don't take it, Lara!" The muffled warning came from Ergot, deep in Barnaby's shirt pocket.

Lara shook her head. "Ergot's right, I can't take it. It would be wrong. I don't understand it beyond bare fundamentals or know how to control its power."

Mag Namodder was impressed at the maturity of Lara's remark. "I would not have told you that," she said, "but what you say is quite true. All right, since you feel that way, I'll keep it for you. One day, when the time is right and you feel ready for it, I shall return it."

She snugged the golden loop of the Wand around her left wrist and when she straightened and let her arms fall naturally, her hand and the Wand were out of sight in the folds of her robe. "Now," she told them, "we still face a great problem."

"That's right," spoke up Quill. "We've got to escape from this place and get back to Mesmeria."

"That is exactly what you should do — all of you," Mag Namodder responded. "There are a number of other Kewprums here in the dungeons. You must release them and they can carry you swiftly back to Mesmeria. I will follow when, and if, my task here is finished."

"But *you* have to come with us," Barnaby protested. "That's what we came all the way here for — to rescue you and the others."

"I wish it were that simple," Mag Namodder replied, "but it's not. If I simply escaped with you, which you've now made possible, we'd probably get back safely, but where would that leave us? Krumpp would still control Mesmeria and remain the same threat to everyone that he is right now. By staying here — on my terms — I may be able to change that."

"And what about his powers?" Kite asked, his worry evident.

"Krumpp's basic powers for evil are no greater than

mine are for good. Yes, he made me powerless once, but that was because I let myself become vulnerable and did not realize at the time the power of his yellow-jeweled ring. In its own way, the Yellow Ring is as powerful for evil as the Wand is for good. Now, thanks to you, Lara, I have the use of the Wand. This time he will not be apt to catch me unawares. And now I have no other alternative — I must face him and try to strip him of his evil powers."

"Then you won't be doing it alone," Lara said quietly. "I'm going with you."

"And so am I," declared Barnaby, moving over beside her.

"Oh, wonderful!" came a sardonic rumble from Barnaby's shirt pocket.

"I'll be going with you, too," said Daw.

One by one, despite the fear they felt, the others all agreed and with no further delay they left the cell, following Mag Namodder.

18

Back to the Great Chamber

EXCEPT FOR THE paralyzed Troll, Centaur and three Warted Gnomes, the dungeon corridor was empty, as were all the cells they passed. The closest of those cells had their heavy doors blown off by Lara's spell; those midway down the corridor were hanging askew, while those toward the end had simply swung open.

They moved cautiously through the long long corridor until they finally reached the foot of the steps where the guards remained paralyzed in full flight. At a nod from Mag Namodder they crept up the extensive flight of steps to the next level. The equally long corridor there was devoid of guards, and Mag Namodder paused and stepped aside, nodding to Lara to do what was required here. The little girl narrowed her eyes and cast a dual spell. The first part of it opened the doors of each of the hundred or more cells, nearly all of them occupied, some with several individuals. The second part telepathically informed the greatly dazed occupants now moving hesitantly into the corridor that they had the option at this time — since they were not spellbound — to flee in an uncontrolled mob up the stairs, or to show their courage and throw their support behind Lara and her brave little cluster of followers. She warned that whatever they could do would have to be accomplished largely without the aid of Mag Namodder, who had a difficult course of her own to follow. Most of the erstwhile prisoners chose the latter course.

By the time this same process was followed at the two remaining dungeon levels above them and they had finally reached the ground level of Black Castle, close to a thousand liberated prisoners were following behind them, noisily chanting, "Lara! Lara! Lara!" Among them were Gnomes and Dwarfs and Centaurs, Tworps and Kewprums and Dwirgs, Trolls and Men and Elves, Dryads and Nyads and Chumplers, Lutras and Drales and Fauns, Satyrs and Freeps and Volers, Ursos and Imps and even a few Tripodians and Krins and Vulpines. But more numerous among the released prisoners than any other creatures were the Blakkrats — hundred upon hundreds of them.

"One might logically assume," Ergot murmured reflectively, "that Krumpp has a considerable dislike for

Blakkrats. That being the case," he mused, "one might wonder why."

Quill, feeling much more confident now that the large makeshift army was behind them, couldn't resist needling the Shrood. "Ergot, ten or fifteen minutes ago I distinctly remember you saying Krumpp was going to show up again in two minutes." He pointed at the empty main corridor stretching out before them. "So where is he?"

"That analysis," replied Ergot huffily, "did not state that Krumpp would show up. It stated that he would be made aware of the situation that was developing in the lower dungeon and implied that within two minutes he would begin preparing remedial measures. Nothing has occurred to change that. It is obvious now that whatever steps he has taken, he probably chooses to confront us where he feels he will have the greatest advantage. So far as we know at this time, that place will be in the Great Chamber where we first encountered him."

"A shrewd deduction, Ergot," chuckled Mag Namodder, "if you'll forgive the pun. And," she added, becoming much more serious, "what you say is probably true. Krumpp is most likely waiting for us in the Great Chamber and we must assume he is fully prepared. At this time he probably wants nothing more than to destroy all of you. I think this is something you should now consider one last time before possibly getting yourselves into an irreversibly deadly situation."

Lara nodded. "I was not able to fully understand the

situation in regard to Krumpp's power against you — or even against me, for that matter — when I first read *The Secret Volumes*. I only sensed he could not execute you. Now I think I am beginning to better understand the strange language and symbolic expression used in those books. It seems to me now that what *The Secret Volumes of Warp* say in their own peculiar way is that under the laws governing sorcery, no sorcerer may kill another, irrespective of provocation. Should he even *try* to do so, the consequences are total forfeiture of all magic abilities. But this ruling does not mean that one sorcerer cannot put another into a situation where he or she will ultimately die of natural causes, as Krumpp attempted to do with you, Mag Namodder. Nor does the ban against inflicting death on others hold true when a sorcerer is dealing with nonsorcerers."

"Exactly," Mag Namodder said, pleased that Lara had figured this out for herself. "Which means that while Krumpp must not try to kill either of *us*, he is not restrained from killing any of the rest of you."

"But he doesn't *know* I'm a sorcerer," Lara said worriedly. "He just thinks I know some simple magic."

"It is every sorcerer's responsibility to recognize another sorcerer when he encounters one, Lara. Now that may be difficult for Krumpp in the case of someone like yourself, who has just become a First Level sorcerer, but it's not impossible and it *is* his responsibility to know. There are no exceptions."

She shook her head. "We're getting away from the point I was making. All of you here," she said, raising her voice slightly so that it carried to every person following her, "are quite likely exposing yourselves to mortal danger. I want you to think it over. In that direction," she pointed up the dimly lighted corridor to a barely visible double door far in the distance, "is the only exit from Black Castle. All who wish to go are now free to leave. In that direction," she pointed down the corridor to another set of double doors barely visible in the distance, "is the Great Chamber, where we will probably have our final confrontation with King Krumpp. That is the direction Lara and I *must* go. But you are *not* required to go. Therefore, the moment has arrived. Make your final choice now."

"We're still with you, Mag Namodder," said Daw, "come what may."

"Not with me," cautioned Mag Namodder, "for what I do cannot involve the assistance of any other. But you *can* assist Lara. Is that your choice?"

"Aye!" came a voice from the crowd following them.

"Yes!" called another.

"Sure!" yelled a third.

"Right!" exclaimed a fourth.

It became a moment of near bedlam as the "ayes" and "yesses" and "sures" and "rights" rose in a crescendo from the hundreds who were gathered. Mag Namodder was deeply moved.

"Whatever occurs," she said earnestly, "I know that Lara will do her utmost to protect you in every way. But you must bear in mind that she is still a very new and inexperienced sorcerer."

With that, she turned and, side by side with Lara, led them down the long main passageway toward the mammoth double doors of the Great Chamber. There they paused once again and, now that the crucial moment had arrived, an uneasy silence settled over them.

"I wonder what we'll find on the other side," Barnaby whispered nervously.

"Krumpp, beyond any doubt," replied Ergot from the boy's pocket, and for once no one asked him how he had come to that conclusion.

"I wonder if he realizes we're out here," said Roo-Too.

"I think *that* answers your question," replied Daw, pointing.

The portal had begun opening . . . to total darkness. To make matters worse, the slow outward swing of the vast iron doors created an awful moany-groany sound, making the whole corridor reverberate with an unnerving banshee wail.

"Tell you what," piped up a frightened voice toward the rear. "There are so many of us, we'll be getting in each other's way. Maybe some of us should wait outside as reinforcements."

"Great idea!" exclaimed another. "I'm with you on that."

"Me, too!" shouted a third.

"Send a messenger if you need us!" yelled another.

A rising chorus of voices agreed and then further words were drowned out by hundreds of feet clattering in a panicky mass exodus toward the far distant exit doors of Black Castle. Before the Great Chamber doors had opened entirely, all but the principal members of the group were gone.

19

Krumpp's Trap

"SO MUCH FOR courage!" came Krumpp's chilling voice. "So much for faith in the powers of the Forest Witch!"

Far across the Great Chamber a pale blue aura sprang into life and expanded, outlining the seated form of King Krumpp on his throne. Unlike the electric blue the aura had been previously, its present wan glow magnified his aspect of malevolence, particularly as everything else remained in darkness.

"Why are you just standing there?" Krumpp went on, taking a small bite from the yellow rod he held. "Come! Approach me. Or can it be that the Underland Witch and her heretofore lucky but now very foolhardy friends are no less afraid than the cowardly rats who have deserted them?"

"Your days of tyranny are over, Krumpp," shouted Daw, his muscles bunching as he prepared to leap toward the blue-lighted figure.

"Don't move!" Mag Namodder cautioned in an undertone. "He's taunting us for a reason."

She raised her right hand, palm forward, fingers outstretched, and spoke a single word. "*Flamma.*"

There was a heavy *whoomp* sound and scores upon scores of brightly flaming torches appeared on the walls at ten-foot intervals all the way around the room. The interior of the Great Chamber was now clearly visible and the only significant change was that the multitude of tables and benches that had covered the whole floor space had now been moved against the walls, leaving the center of the stone floor open, like a ballroom. There were no fewer people than previously and they all lined the perimeter of the vast room. As before, by far the greater number were Blakkrats.

The appearance of light in the room dazzled its occupants, some of whom were sitting on the benches and tables, and they stirred uncomfortably, blinked rapidly and shielded their eyes until they could grow accustomed to it; but none made any attempt to leave.

"What did you expect," Krumpp laughed, "a Dragon in the middle of the room? You must know I wouldn't do that. I merely wish to talk with you. I'm calling a truce. Take careful note — none of my people here are bearing arms." The initial taunting quality had left his voice and he spoke earnestly. "Look, I've been reconsidering things and am willing to admit that perhaps I've made a few slight errors in my time —"

"Such as conquering Mesmeria?" Daw growled angrily.

"Such as killing people?" Kestra shrieked angrily.

"Such as tyrannizing all who still live there?" put in Kite angrily.

"Such as keeping Mag Namodder and her friends in a dungeon for seven and a half centuries?" interjected Quill, his voice thick with fury.

"Tsk, tsk, tsk," clucked Krumpp with mild admonishment, biting another chunk from the yellow rod. "Is such vituperation really necessary? After all, I admit I've made mistakes. Let bygones by bygones, eh? Forgive and forget? Mag Namodder, listen to me, it's altogether foolish for there to be any further antagonism between us. Surely we can agree to coexist." He smiled and beckoned. "Come, let us reason together."

Mag Namodder studied him quietly for a moment and then her lips quirked in a faint smile. "Yes," she said, "reasoning together might be beneficial, but why don't *you* come to *us*? Allow me to assist you." She dipped her head toward him and said, "*Attrahent!*"

Without getting up, Krumpp started toward them, but it was not of his own volition. The jewel-studded throne upon which he was sat was moving. And the reason the throne was moving was because the intricately carved wooden dais upon which the throne rested had begun sliding toward the center of the room in the direction of Mag Namodder and her party. Krumpp's expression became fearful as he tried to get to his feet, but could not.

"Stop it!" he cried. "You can't kill me — it's forbidden."

"But how am I trying to kill you, Krumpp?" Mag Namodder asked innocently. "I am only moving you toward us so we may, as you put it, reason together."

The King's eyes bulged as he strained at the force pinning him into his throne, but he could not break away by physical strength alone.

"*Recule!*" he shrieked.

The spell thrust his entire throne backward, tumbling it off the rear of the dais and sending him rolling end over end out of the chair. The dais, however, continued forward, but not for long. As it reached the center of the chamber it suddenly tilted up on edge and disappeared through the floor. In a few seconds there came the sound of a tremendous splash from far below and then the piercing, rattling shrieks characteristic of the dreaded Grinjels.

"Krumpp!" Mag Namodder pointed at him as he scrambled to his feet, his blue aura even more faded.

"You invited us to come forward to speak in truce. That was treachery! The center floor is an illusion. We would have fallen into the shaft and been killed by Grinjels."

"Ah, but not *you*, Mag Namodder!" He grinned wickedly at her. "Do not take me for a fool. Zitt stood prepared to catch you, and we both know he would not have missed. Behold!"

Krumpp thrust out his right hand and staggered slightly as a broad ray of amber light from the Yellow Ring on his thumb illuminated the floor in a ten-foot circle. What appeared to be the floor shimmered and then vanished — an illusion, as Mag Namodder had said — leaving the gaping mouth of a pit as neatly formed as the inside of a silo. And, on a platform just below floor level crouched Zitt — a crepuscular Krin — his twenty-five-foot tail tightly coiled over his reptilian back, his jagged teeth exposed in a hideous grin.

Mag Namodder was grudgingly impressed, and now realized why the evil sorcerer's aura was so dim. She understood the enormous amount of spell-power it must have taken for Krumpp to set up this elaborate trap in so short a time. To start with, the King had had to create the pit from this floor level all the way down through the mountain to below water level and then capture and transport the Grinjels to put in it. More of his power was drained in creating the realistic illusion of the stone floor over its opening. Little wonder, then, that he had staggered slightly just now when he removed the illusory floor to prove he had not tried to kill Mag Namodder.

She shook her head sadly. "You are more a fool than you realize, Krumpp. You might not actually have tried to kill *me*," she glanced toward Lara, "but this child —"

"*SORDO!*" screamed Krumpp, taking instant advantage of her eyes being off him.

Krumpp had exerted a great deal of his remaining energy into the silencing command. Yet, that alone would not have been enough, for her powers were at this point much more than equal to his and she could have thwarted it. But at the same time he had shoved his hand toward her and a pencil-thin beam of yellow light streaked from the jeweled thumb-ring and hit her full in the face, causing the power of his spell to be multiplied many times over.

Abruptly unable to speak, Mag Namodder began raising the Wand toward Krumpp, but she never finished the movement. There was a swishing, whistling sound followed by a loud bang that echoed through the chamber like the crack of a rifle . . . and Mag Namodder crumpled as if she had been shot, the Wand flying from her grip and skidding across the floor before finally coming to a stop actually teetering on the rim of the pit.

Because of where each had been positioned, Barnaby, Ergot and Zitt had had the best perspective of what happened. Zitt, perched on the rickety platform below the lip of the pit, saw Krumpp reel from the effect of the *Sordo* spell and he also saw Mag Namodder begin to lift the Wand. With blurring speed his tail shot out and, like some incredible bullwhip, it snapped at her head. Krins seldom miss their mark, and the cracking tip has the power to snap off a limb or a head without difficulty. But Zitt's unstable platform lurched just at that moment and the tail missed Mag Namodder's head by the merest fraction, cracking the air close to her with such concussion that it knocked her insensible.

Barnaby didn't know this; he only saw her fall. With Ergot in his pocket yelling excited encouragement, the boy bellowed with rage and leaped forward. He snatched at the Krin's tail and, before it could be re-coiled, bit it as hard as he could. At the same time, Kite leaped into the air and fluttered to assist him. Kestra sped through the air toward Krumpp, while Rana Pipian charged him on the floor. Roo-Too rushed to aid Mag Namodder and Lara scrambled toward the edge of the pit after the precariously balanced Wand from one direction, while Krumpp plunged toward it from the other. For the moment, Quill and Daw stood rooted.

The Krin named Zitt jerked and roared with mingled pain and rage as Barnaby's teeth sank into his tail, but the roar turned into a hoarse scream as his jerking around caused him to lose his balance and fall. His scream lasted with rapidly diminishing volume until he hit the water and then was overwhelmed by the louder, more terrifying, rattling shrieks of the Grinjels as they devoured him. But Zitt's initial jerk as his tail was bitten had caused the whiplike appendage to smack Barnaby a glancing blow across the shoulders, almost dislodging Ergot from the pocket and sending the boy sprawling. Barnaby rolled to the edge of the pit and then fell inside. He landed on the planking where Zitt had been perched and the platform creaked and cracked and tore free from its supports on one end. Ergot shrieked and clung desperately to the buttonhole, while Barnaby wound up hanging upside down, swaying, suspended by one foot. A broken beam snapped free and slid past, its jagged end scraping him in its passage, scoring his skin as if he had been clawed by a vicious beast, ripping away his shirt and plummeting with it toward the bottom of the pit. Again the Grinjels screeched. And still Barnaby hung there.

He sobbed then, deeply, convulsively. Even though Daw, Quill and Kite quickly reached the edge and pulled him to safety, he continued to cry. They thought it was because of the injury he had suffered, but he shook his head. "My . . . shirt. It's gone!"

"That's nothing to cry over," Quill said, surprised at such concern.

"You don't understand. You just don't *understand!* Ergot was in my pocket. He's *gone!*"

And then the others wept with him.

Everything seemed to be happening in slow motion.

All these things had taken place in just a few seconds and the occurrences were not yet over. Krumpp had warded off the charge of Kestra and Rana Pipian with a weak bolt of yellow light from his ring, leaving them stunned. But the time it took him to do that foiled his intention of kicking the Wand into the pit. Instead, Lara managed to snatch it up and race away toward Roo-Too and Mag Namodder. Krumpp, momentarily off balance, recovered his equilibrium and his gaze went to Lara. She, with Roo-Too, was bending over Mag Namodder, trying to help her.

"You!" the King snarled, pointing at Lara. "You're the cause of all this trouble! You stole *The Secret Volumes of Warp*. You led your friends here and you brought Mag Namodder back to health and power. And now you've got that Wand!" He drew his rapier from its scabbard as he advanced on her. "I should've killed you before. I certainly will now!"

Lara sprang to her feet just as he began his final lunge toward her, the deadly point of the rapier aimed directly at her heart.

"*Phantos!*"

She raised the Wand as the spell-word sprang from her lips. In that fraction of time it took Krumpp's lethal blade to plunge the final inches to her chest, her body became evanescent, shimmery, without material substance. The blade struck . . . and passed through. And, because of his momentum and the lack of resistance met at his thrust, so did Krumpp's hand and his arm and then his entire body as he stumbled through the apparition that had moments before been flesh and blood.

He caught himself without having fallen and spun about, aghast. By then, Lara, substantial again, had turned and was facing him. For the two of them, this moment had become a separated time; one that encompassed only them; nothing else — no one else — existed. He stared at her and what he saw was happiness, but also sorrow; he saw triumph, but also compassion; he saw innocence and, at the same time, infinite wisdom.

He saw Lara.

And he knew . . . he *knew!*

"You . . . you're . . . you're a sorcerer!"

She nodded.

"And I . . . I tried to kill you."

Again she nodded.

The aura that had surrounded Krumpp vanished. As did the form of Krumpp itself, for that form had only been an illusion; the form he had taken for himself over a millennium ago, when his mentor, Warp, had considered it a gigantic jest to teach such a lowly creature the mysteries of sorcery. Krumpp's clothing plopped into a pile as his body reverted to its original form. The Yellow Ring dropped free and clinked to the floor, bounced and rolled and then dropped into the Grinjel pit. The final yellow rod from which he had been nibbling fell half-eaten to the stone floor.

Barnaby approached, limping, helped along by Quill and Daw and Kite. Kestra and Rana Pipian followed. Still slightly dazed and aided by Roo-Too, Mag Namodder joined them from the other direction. They all converged where Lara was standing and stared, as she was doing, at the residue of what had been Krumpp.

"He tried to kill you, Lara," said Mag Namodder.

It was not a question, but the girl nodded.

"Who — or what — do you suppose he was, really?" Barnaby asked.

An answer was unnecessary. There was a movement under the pile of clothing and a small creature poked its head out, then emerged all the way. It sat up on its haunches and regarded them in a vacant manner, then dropped to all fours. Its twitching nose led it to where the partially eaten yellow rod lay on the stone floor. It paused and nibbled eagerly from the rod and probably would have stayed there longer, but an excited chattering made it look up and it stiffened with fear.

The hundreds of Blakkrats on the benches and tables along the perimeter of the room were not very bright, but it had finally gotten through to them that the Krumpp Empire had ended at last and they flocked in an enthusiastic crowd toward the little group of adventurers who had freed them from tyranny. The little creature saw them coming and he dropped the cheese stick he had been nibbling upon and scurried into a crack in the stone floor to hide from his hereditary enemies.

And that was the last anyone ever saw of the mouse named Krumpp.

Epilogue

Why have you turned to this page? Didn't you realize only a moment ago that the story of the Wand ended on the previous page?

Well, it did, so you can just turn out the light and snuggle down and go to sleep now.

What?

. . . Well, imagine that! You say you still need to know some things or you'll never get to sleep tonight?

You want to know what happened to Daw and Roo-Too?

. . . and Quill and Kestra and Kite?

. . . and Mag Namodder?

. . . Oh! And, most of all, what happened to Lara and Barnaby?

Okay. I certainly wouldn't want to spoil your rest, so I guess a brief concluding summary might not be out of order.

You do understand, of course, that Lara and Barnaby had no intention of staying in Mesmeria (once they'd returned there after the trouble had ended) because they hadn't even planned on being back there again so soon. And they hated to think of their mother and stepfather waiting too much longer for them at Chicago's O'Hare Airport even if time were not really passing for them. So, after things at Black Castle had settled down and a benevolent, very wise old Warted Gnome named Trukk was elected to succeed Krumpp as the new leader of Bluggia, the members of the party — along with a very large number of former prisoners of the Black Castle dungeons who wanted to go with them — set out for Mesmeria.

What a spectacle they made! Including Kestra and Kite, there were thirty Kewprums, but strong as they were, they were certainly not enough to carry everyone back to Mesmeria who wanted to go. That was when Mag Namodder had appealed to the leader of the Vulpines — which, in itself, was a surprise to many, since hardly anybody thought the Vulpines were intelligent enough to even have a leader.

Anyway, his name was Belcher and Mag Namodder convinced him to agree to a truce and have three full squadrons of Vulpines carry the survivors of the Black Castle dungeons back to Mesmeria. And that's just what they did. Each of the Vulpines could carry a very heavy load and so the Dwarfs and Centaurs and Tworps and Dwirgs and all the others crowded on their backs and, with the thirty Kewprums leading the way, they flew south.

Once they had crossed the totally dark area and then crossed the breadth of Dymzonia and entered Mesmeria, the sky became very bright. The returning survivors were overjoyed at seeing the Mesmerian sun again, but not the Vulpines, many of whom had never been south of their own borders before. At last the Vulpines refused to go farther. They landed in northern Rubiglen and their passengers disembarked. Some continued homeward on the backs of the Kewprums and others on the backs of the Centaurs and even more continued on foot and they all got home safely.

The word of Mesmeria's liberation spread quickly to every reach of Rubiglen and Selerdor and Mellafar and Verdancia, and the occupying troops were given amnesty and allowed to stay or return to their own homes, whichever they chose. Most decided to go home and in only a few days hardly any remained.

It was a time of great celebration throughout Mesmeria. Daw and Roo-Too were immediately reinstated as King and Queen of Mesmeria and they and their subjects clamored for Barnaby and Lara to resume joint rule as well, for the twins were greatly loved by all. But the two respectfully declined, wanting very much to get home this time without any further delay.

A beautiful bronze plaque was cast that memorialized the heroic and deeply loved Ergot who had been lost, and a statue of him, ten times life size, was raised in the beautiful grassy glen that was ever afterward to be known as Ergot-the-Shrood Park.

Quill finally returned to the foothills of the Ruby Mountains where he built a nice cozy cottage in a lovely meadow not far from the home of his friends, Skaz and Ursha, and Skaz promised to teach Quill how to prospect for gemstones.

Kestra and Kite were soon joined by Kite's brother, Pere-Grin. On the backs of these three beautiful Kewprums, Mag Namodder, Barnaby and Lara returned to Twilandia. A gala welcome awaited them and already work was in progress to rebuild Mag Namodder's palace and the city of Fir Tree and to restore the farms to their former beauty. It was a task made far more enjoyable when Mag Namodder, using the Wand, restored the life-giving brilliance to the clouds of Twilandia . . . even though the effort took so much energy that she required weeks thereafter to recuperate.

Since returning from Bluggia, Barnaby had been wearing an extra shirt Quill had given him — to replace the one he had lost, with Ergot in the pocket — but it was too small and quite uncomfortable. At Mag Namodder's request, a dozen Fairies wove him a new shirt from the ultra-soft, pale blue fuzz of Mesmerian dandelions. It was an intricate and very distinctive weave and by far the most beautiful and comfortable shirt Barnaby had ever owned.

It was Kite and Kestra who sadly agreed to carry the twins part of the way on the final leg of their journey home. With the farewells of the crowds rising all about them — and the twins' own promises to return just as soon as possible — the beautiful hawks took off and carried Lara and Barnaby in majestic flight to the very ledge of the Twilandia Cliffs where this adventure had begun for them.

"It's so nice to be with people you love and who love you in return," Lara said, sniffling, "and so sad to have to say good-bye."

"Yes," Barnaby said, wiping his eyes with the heels of his hands so he could get one last glimpse of Kite and Kestra soaring back toward Fir Tree. In a moment he glanced back at Lara and then put his arm around her shoulders. "C'mon," he said softly, "let's go home."

They walked through the arched tunnelway and into the cavernous chamber of the Spelunkens, marveling once more at the beauty of the stalagmites and stalactites. They tried to rouse Rock and bid him farewell, but he merely changed the pitch of his snoring a little and refused to awaken.

The journey up the slippery steps and slicker upward incline of the cave was more difficult than when they had descended, but eventually the passage became drier and more level. Still, they walked and walked and the cave remained a cave and did not become an airport corridor as they had expected. They began getting a little apprehensive but then, as they turned a bend, they jolted to a halt. The cave came to a dead end — or at least they thought it was, until they saw the ordinary door with a box mounted on the wall beside it.

Lara opened the door and peeked out. A gleaming tiled passageway was there and at an intersecting corridor only a dozen yards ahead was a large sign in the shape of an arrow pointing down the left corridor. On it were lettered the words:

BAGGAGE CLAIM

"We've found it, Barnaby!" she exclaimed. "Look!"

When he didn't answer immediately, she turned back and saw that he had lifted the lid of the box on the wall, which was something like a fire alarm box. Lara frowned.

"I don't think you're supposed to fool with that," she warned.

"Sure, it's okay, Lara. Look here."

He lowered the lid and on the outside were two words:

Please Open

"Now look at what's inside," he added, lifting the lid again.

She craned her neck to look and saw there was a tiny screen there, not even a quarter the size of a microcomputer screen. It was flashing three words — green letters on a dark background:

Please Press Button

"Well, what do you think, Lara? Should we?"

"I don't know," she replied slowly. She shook her head. "No, I don't think so."

"Hey," he urged, "it says 'Please Press Button' and I'm going to."

He did . . . and immediately the screen changed to a new set of words:

Silly!
Do you always blindly do anything
anybody tells you to do?

There was a heavy rumbling then. Bits of debris began falling from the cave roof and the rumbling grew more thunderous. Lara gave a frightened cry.

"Barnaby! Let's get out of here. Hurry!"

They leaped through the door and slammed it closed just as the entire ceiling of the tunnel caved in. The door shook and rattled violently and then the rumbling faded away. Very tentatively, Barnaby opened the door. The only thing visible was a solid wall of rubble. Shaking his head in bewilderment, he closed it again. Lara tapped his shoulder and he looked at her and then at where she was pointing.

On the wall next to the door was a large neatly lettered sign:

CONSTRUCTION AREA — KEEP OUT

* * *

Another expansion by the City of Chicago
to meet the needs of a growing America

* * *

"Well, Lara," Barnaby said regretfully, shrugging, "I guess there's no chance we'll ever get back to Mesmeria again this way."

"Maybe not this way, Barnaby," she responded, pointing at the arrow sign, "but come on. I'll bet Mother will know a way."

. . . And you know what? Lara was right.

But, you see, that's another story.

The End

MELANISTICA
DARKLAND

TEMPEST OCEAN

BLUGGIA

Blackrat Riv.
Bay of Nightmares
Bluggburg
GREAT UNKN
Black Castle
Grunda Is.
CHALKYN
Kite Riv.
KESTRA Riv.
ergot's ledge
Lona's Needle Rock

D Y M Z

Phalco R.
Lake of Tears
DESO

RUBUGLEEZ

Red Lake
Dawburg
Amethyst Lake
Ruby Mts.
Rose Lake
Red Sand Hills
SELER
Cherry Soda Lake
Crescent Bay

VERDIA
Green Lake
Gray Mts.
MELLAFAR
Blue Mountains